love bites hard

MATED TO THE KING

LOLA GLASS

Cover by Francesca Michelon
https://www.merrybookround.com/

To my husband
For loving me even though I change my mind constantly

one

IZZY

I GRIPPED Clementine's arm like a lifeline as we walked down the cold, modern hallways of Vamp Manor. Her pale skin was growing pink beneath my touch, and a few strands of her long, wet red hair were trapped under my fingers, but neither of us cared.

I needed to act like I was unfazed by what was about to happen, even if it wasn't true.

Zora grabbed my other arm. Her collarbone-length, curly brown hair was up in a bun that dripped water onto her tan shoulders as she fell into step with me and Clem. "You can still say no."

She was right.

I *could* still say no.

But I wasn't going to.

As a siren, I was one of the weakest kinds of magical beings that existed. Not that *my* magic was weak. I was normal.

But siren magic was useless in a fight, only serving to pull people in and make them feel good when I tapped into it.

Which meant I was in danger.

Constantly.

My four sisters were in the same boat, too.

The best way to protect yourself as a siren was to take a strong mate. My sister Blair had done exactly that, though she'd done it to keep all of us safe. The vampire king she'd mated with would protect us—but not from everything.

There was a wolf shifter after Clementine, and the only way to get rid of him for good was to have *another* wolf rip his throat out.

Hence my upcoming nuptials with a stronger wolf.

Starting a mate bond with the wolf was my decision. And it wasn't one I was going back on.

Technically, my sisters and I could've just stayed with the vampires forever, but we would've spent the rest of our lives in danger. Trapped in Vamp Manor.

While some of my sisters loved the vampires, I wasn't the biggest fan. They were fine, but something about blood drinking gave me the creeps.

Maybe it was the teeth.

Or the biting.

Or feeding on people.

Considering sirens drank emotions by kissing, I was a total hypocrite. But it was what it was.

And I was ready to get some space from the vampires.

Mating with a wolf shifter definitely wasn't the *smartest* way to escape from the vamps. But it was the only way that would ensure both my safety and my sisters', so it seemed like a win-win situation.

Minus the mate bond part.

But there were worse things than being mated to a hot werewolf dude, weren't there?

I was going with yes.

Anyway, the agreement was simple:

I would seal a mate bond with Porter Jenkins.

Then, he would challenge the alpha werewolf who was trying to take my sister. Curtis was his name.

After Porter killed Curtis, we'd live happily ever after.

Or at least, we would *live*.

Together, potentially?

I wasn't quite sure what came after the killing part.

But Porter would be the new wolf king, AKA alpha. He wanted my magic's help to get him out of the funk he'd been in since he lost his family.

So, the *living* part would happen, and that was what mattered.

"Should we put clothes on before we do this?" Avery, another one of my sisters, murmured. She had olive skin, and her dark brown hair was tied up at the base of her neck, dripping just as much as the rest of ours.

We'd just gotten out of the pool, so all of us were wearing our bikinis. Blair, my only mated sister, had her mate's button-up shirt on over her swimsuit. Her skin was light and her hair golden, falling down to the middle of her back in tangled, wet waves.

Sirens loved water. Swimsuits were worn frequently, but something to put on over the top of them rarely crossed our minds. Which meant I was meeting my mate in nothing but my sporty black bikini.

"Nah. Maybe if I let Porter see the goods, he'll have more of a reason to get through his fight with Curtis," I said, adjusting the straps of my suit so more of my boobs were on display. My skin was light brown, and my naturally platinum-blonde hair was even more of a tangled mess than Blair's.

"You're literally insane," Blair grumbled, her hand locked with Hale's. That was a mate perk I guess, though I didn't think I'd ever be able to hold someone's hand like she was without feeling ridiculous.

Her mate was gorgeous. Damian Hale was a gigantic vampire with light skin and messy, dark hair. All magical men were big, but he took it to the next level.

"Says the woman who mated with the vampire king to save all of our asses in the first place," I drawled.

"But our asses are *saved*, aren't they?" she pointed out. "You're sacrificing yourself for no reason."

"You saved us. I'm freeing us."

Really, I was freeing myself.

It was selfish, but I couldn't stay trapped inside Vamp Manor for another day.

So many predators.

So many teeth.

"The wolves have even more teeth," Zora pointed out.

I must've said that last bit aloud.

"They don't bite people as often," I said.

We were nearly to Hale's office, where Porter was waiting.

My stomach was so tight, the damn thing may as well have been a rock.

"Wolves still bite their mates," Hale remarked.

Before I could ask him what he meant, or even really process his words, the door in front of us opened and a man stepped out.

My attention went straight to him.

He was already staring at me.

And somehow, he was just as big as Hale.

His skin was tan, his wavy reddish-brown hair an utter catastrophe. It was shaved on the sides, which I liked, but I could see the point of a leaf sticking out of the top part. His hair was so thick, I could imagine he hadn't even realized the leaf was there.

He was stunning, but in a completely different way than Hale was.

Where Hale was put-together, Porter was wild.

Untamed.

Absolutely, entirely unpolished.

His black sweats and gray t-shirt were wrinkled, and I could see a streak of dirt on one of his shoulders.

Even without talking to him, I could tell the man was nothing like the vampires.

And that alone made me want to walk right into his stupidly gigantic arms.

"We should've split up so he didn't see all of us," Avery murmured.

"Whoops," Clementine whispered back.

"If he's mating with me, he's going to be around you guys sometimes," I said to them, still unable to look away from the giant in the doorway of Hale's office.

Maybe it was my pride, but I wanted him to know he was mating with *me*. I didn't want him checking out one of my sisters, or wishing he'd gotten paired with someone else.

"He'll keep the secret," Hale agreed.

"It's not a secret. Curtis has told everyone how many sirens you're hiding, even if you refuse to admit it to the other kings," Porter said, his voice deeper and much more gravelly than I could remember from the phone call I'd listened to between him and Hale.

"He'll play along," Blair corrected.

Porter's eyes didn't leave me, but he nodded once.

"Should we make this into a ceremony or something?" Clementine joked, as we finally stopped in front of him.

"No," Porter said flatly. "I'm going to talk to my mate alone."

With that, he grabbed me by the waist and tugged me into the office, shutting and locking the door behind me.

My back was pinned to it a moment later, with who-knew-how-many pounds of delicious male muscle less than a breath away from me. The man towered over me, and my toes curled immediately.

The rough and tumble thing?

It worked for me.

Really, really worked for me.

"Let me feel your magic," he said.

It wasn't a command, exactly, but he didn't make it sound optional.

"You can't order me around. You're not *my* alpha," I shot back, irritated by his immediate need to take control.

"If you want me to challenge the alpha of Mistwood, you're going to have to let me feel your magic to prove what you are before I mate with you," he growled.

I huffed... but it was a fair point.

And though I could've just pushed my magic out at him, I didn't want to give him exactly what he wanted.

I wanted to prove that I wasn't going to be a pushover.

So I grabbed his face, pulling him toward me as I went up on my tiptoes and kissed him.

Porter's mouth was soft against mine, despite the roughness of his appearance. He grabbed my waist as I pulled his emotions into me, and he parted his lips on a sharp inhale at the feel of my power.

My tongue dragged against his lightly, and he launched into action, kissing me hard and fast.

Desperately.

Like I was the air he needed to breathe.

And the man was *delicious*.

Shallow feelings were like junk food for a siren—fun, but not filling.

Deeper, more intense emotions?

They were homemade bread. Pot roast. Steak and potatoes.

The bigger meals that we craved and needed.

And Porter?

He was a buffet.

A siren's wet dream.

Pain.

Hatred.

Sadness.

Despair.

Agony.

Emptiness.

The tiniest flicker of hope.

He pushed me away suddenly, and my back thudded against the door as his mouth was ripped away from mine.

My chest rose and fell quickly. My lips tingled from the brutality of our kiss, and my blood pumped hard with the immensity of the emotions I'd taken from him.

"Don't ever feed from me without permission," he snarled, though it didn't hold nearly as much heat as the growl he'd given me before I kissed him.

He was scrambling for his anger, trying to rebuild the dam over his intense emotions before anything else slid free.

"What happened to you?" I asked, unable to stop myself.

"I'm not looking for a therapist." He stepped closer, wrapping his hand around my throat. My heart beat against his fingers, and he froze for a moment, feeling the rapid thud.

Ba-dum.

Ba-dum.

Ba-dum.

Ba-dum.

"You shouldn't mate with a siren if you're not ready to work through your emotions," I said honestly. "I'm going to have to feed on you twice a week to stay strong."

His lips twisted in a snarl, but it was halfhearted. And finally, he said the magic words that would start a mate bond between us. "You are mine."

"You don't even know my name," I breathed, as the binding magic rolled through my body, warming and electrifying me all at once.

Shit, I hoped he pictured something pretty. The mate bond's magic naturally resembled a thick bar around both parties' necks unless they crafted something better in their mind. Call me shallow, but I wanted something *nice* around my throat for all of eternity.

It was too late for that, though.

"I don't need to know your name," he said, not yet releasing his hold on me.

"You're an asshole." I grabbed him by the throat too, digging my nails in just enough to make his eyes narrow. "If you didn't make the mark on my throat look nice, you're in for a lifetime of blue balls."

"This isn't about sex."

"I didn't say it was. But you are *mine*, too."

The magic of our shiny new mate bond becoming permanent sent tingles through my body.

I focused on giving him a mark that matched mine, whatever the hell it looked like, and watched closely as a delicate, looping band wrapped around his throat.

The tension in my shoulders eased as it did.

At least he wasn't a *total* bastard.

"And if you don't want me screwing someone else, there *will* be sex," I said, digging my nails in a little deeper before I finally released him and stepped away from the door. My chest met his, and he growled at me again.

I opened the door behind me and walked back through, trying hard to fight whatever the intense emotions pounding through me were. "Now, we have an alpha challenge to get to."

two

PORTER

MY MATE WAS GOING to be the death of me.

I'd survived losing everyone and everything—yet the woman I'd just tied my life to could tear my mind apart with a single sentence.

"If you don't want me screwing someone else, there will be sex."

I didn't have any idea who she could be picturing herself in bed with, but I was already vividly imagining myself tearing him apart limb by limb.

Wolves didn't share.

She was mine.

She was fucking *mine*.

Any other bastard who touched her would be dead before he had time to enjoy the feel of her perfect little body in his hands.

I snarled quietly, earning weird looks from nearly all of her sisters.

Hale was smirking.

I itched to break his nose with my fist, but he, at the very least, was no threat. A vampire wouldn't even consider drinking from someone who wasn't his blood mate after he'd met his, and sex rarely happened without blood drinking for them.

That I knew of, at least.

But I hadn't been around vampires in so long that I couldn't be sure.

Hell, I hadn't been around my *friend* in so long that I couldn't be sure.

Not that I'd been around anyone else, either.

I clenched my fists.

I needed to focus on the fight with Curtis.

After that, I could figure out what to do with my siren.

three

IZZY

I'D BARELY SAID goodbye to my sisters when a literal wall of vampire men encircled me. They were so huge, I couldn't see over them. They stood so tightly in a circle that I couldn't see through them, either.

They walked down what I thought was a hallway, basically dragging me along between them. It was intensely uncomfortable, but it was better than being handed over to the wolves, so I dealt with it.

We entered what seemed to be a massive room with insanely high ceilings, and finally, I could see something.

Bleachers.

So many bleachers.

They looked like they'd been dragged in, and were set up in a massive circle around something in the middle of the room that the vampires were blocking from my view. It didn't take a rocket scientist to realize it was probably Porter and Curtis, since everyone was there to see them fight.

My guards led me to the bottom of the bleachers. They could've let me stand on one of the benches, but instead kept me on the tile floor.

And closed in around me even tighter.

I fought the urge to push them away.

They were there for my benefit, even if it didn't feel like it.

When I tried to peek through the small gaps between them, I caught glimpses of a cage in front of me.

The room grew progressively louder until the bleachers were full. Then, someone with a microphone commanded everyone to shut up.

He announced that the challenge for alpha would only have one winner—and that whoever didn't win, would die.

My eyes widened.

That was a *lovely* little piece of information.

I should've asked for more details about wolf challenges before I went and bound myself to Porter.

What if he lost, and died?

Holy crap, I could be spending the rest of my immortal life alone.

Granted, I could probably find people to keep me company. Our mate bond would prevent me from feeding on anyone but him, but if he died, I'd be free from that.

I wouldn't be able to bond with anyone else.

But I'd figure it out. It'd be fine.

Probably.

Forcing a slow breath out, I fought the tension in my stomach as the microphone guy announced the start of the fight.

The vampires were still blocking my view. I didn't know if that made my stress worse, or better.

I wouldn't see my shiny new mate lose... but I also wouldn't see if he won. And that felt like something I should be allowed to see, given our relationship.

But all things considered, it did seem safer to stay hidden. Especially if Porter was about to die.

The crowd roared and cheered.

I didn't know who they were in favor of, but their excitement told me that he was winning.

Or maybe they just liked watching people fight, and didn't care who won. That wouldn't particularly surprise me. I didn't know enough about wolf shifters to say that for sure, though.

Gasps went through the crowd, and I went up on my tiptoes, trying to see what was happening.

A brutal snapping noise made me flinch, but the crowd absolutely went crazy. They screamed and hollered.

Someone had just died.

I hadn't felt anything, despite our mate bond, which made me think that it wasn't Porter.

Sure enough, the vampires around me finally parted, and my gaze landed on my new mate.

He was naked.

Bloody and bleeding just about everywhere, too.

But he was alive, and that was more of a relief than I expected.

I spared a glance at Curtis's body on the ground, making a noise of surprise when my attention jerked back to Porter.

He strode across the cage that separated the crowd from the fight, climbing over the wall and dropping to the ground smoothly, only a few feet from me.

My vampire guards cleared out as the gigantic wolf shifter turned me away from him and grabbed my hand. He pumped it into the air as he roared his victory with the crowd, his thick, strong chest against my back.

It was the most bizarre, surreal experience of my life.

But like I said, I didn't know enough about wolves to be certain whether or not it was normal.

Before the crowd's roaring died down, I felt a sharp pain in my shoulder—and choked back a cry when I realized it was Porter's teeth, biting into my skin.

Like a vampire.

It didn't hurt nearly as much as I would've expected, and I was too stunned to shove him off me. His grip was too tight anyway.

He released my shoulder, and roared again with his feral crowd.

Then, without further ado, he tossed me over his shoulder like a sack of potatoes.

I fought the urge to pound my fists into his back and demand he put me down. I wasn't a toddler, and I was the moron who thought it was a good idea to mate with a wolf shifter.

Clearly, I should've asked more questions.

But the hole had been dug and my body was buried, because the mark on my neck wasn't going anywhere. I was stuck with the wolfy bastard for life, and beyond.

And there was nothing I could do about it.

PORTER CARRIED me out of the challenge room and down so many halls that I started to feel a bit dizzy.

The ache in my shoulder wasn't helping with that any.

I could tell when we finally made it into the wolves' wing of the Manor, because the colors of the flooring and walls changed.

The Manor was basically a small city, with a giant building in the center that was considered neutral territory. None of the kings owned that—or all of them did. There were five more wings of the building connected to it, each of them just as large, if not larger, than the center part.

The neutral territory was done in beige colors that were meant to feel luxurious. In contrast, the vampire wing was striking, and everything looked expensive but felt much colder.

I was pleasantly surprised when I saw the flooring change as we entered the wolf wing. It was still tile, but it was dark brown tile that was designed to look like wood. The walls were a warm shade of off-white, and I saw massive landscape photos on the walls we passed.

If my room looked like the hallways, I'd be much more comfortable there than I was in Vamp Manor.

The crowd behind us made me less comfortable, though. It seemed to go on forever, and the noise was insanely loud.

Considering how dizzy I was already feeling, their noise wasn't helping anything.

I expected Porter to take me to his bedroom or something. Instead, he wove through half a dozen massive hallways, then stepped out into the forest. There was a huge clearing just outside the doors, and then there were trees. So many trees.

Some tension in my chest eased as I breathed fresh air.

I had always loved being outside. Even when there wasn't any amount of nature to get lost in, being stuck inside made me feel trapped. The outdoors felt like freedom.

And despite the wolf shifters pouring out of the Manor behind us, I did feel freer without walls around me.

Porter carried me further from the monstrous building, up to the edge of the forest, before he turned around and faced the growing crowd.

I was still hanging off his shoulder, my face pointed to the trees. My dizziness had gotten worse, and I wasn't sure I could stand even if I wanted to. I was starting to think it had something to do with him biting me.

The noise grew louder as we stood where we were for the next handful of minutes.

My vision was so unfocused that I had to concentrate on staying upright on Porter's back rather than trying to figure out why we were waiting.

I had no idea how much time had passed when Porter finally spoke. He didn't yell, shout, or otherwise raise his voice—but somehow, I heard him more clearly than I had ever heard anything.

"I am the new alpha," he said, authority ringing in his voice. "And I will not tolerate any of the behaviors the pack has adopted since Curtis unlawfully took my place. Our pack protects the Manor, our territory, and most importantly, each other. Anyone who feels otherwise can leave now.

Acting against the pack will be seen as a threat, and will be dealt with accordingly. By me."

A moment of silence passed as he waited for an argument or protest to break out, but no one said a word.

He finally said, "When the moon rises, we'll have a bonfire with Curtis's things. After they've burned to ash, we'll run together. As one."

Cheers and roars erupted again.

My dizziness had grown into intense nausea.

Porter strode back through the deafening crowd, and they parted for him.

I wrestled with my sickness all the way back to the Manor. Through the hallways, too.

When Porter finally stepped into a dim room and set me down on my feet, my gaze locked on a bathroom door, and I ran.

My knees kissed the tile as the contents of my stomach came back up. My hands and arms were on the toilet seat, which may or may not have been clean, but I was too sick to care.

Rough fingers gathered my hair away from my face and off my neck as I vomited again, and again. His hand landed on my shoulder, anchoring me.

"What did you do to me?" I panted, after a particularly violent wave of nausea.

"Brought you into the pack."

"*What?*"

"An alpha can bring any kind of magical being into his pack's mental bond with a bite," he said. "Most magical beings could refuse to allow it to develop, but because you're my mate, you can't stop it. You just have to ride it out."

I wanted to snap at him—but was too busy puking my guts out.

A door opened somewhere in the room, and I vaguely heard footsteps.

"I've got Powerade, crackers, and a few other things," a feminine voice said. "Evan left to get her bags from the vampires."

"Thank you."

I stopped puking for long enough to rest my head on the toilet seat, panting as I tried to catch my breath.

The nausea hadn't faded any, so I knew the break would be a short one. I was vomiting bile, so I wasn't sure how much longer it could go on before I just straight-up passed out.

Thick fingers combed my hair back lightly, then tugged on the strands for a moment before I felt all the hair being tied back in a low bun.

Porter stepped away from me, the warmth of his hand leaving my shoulder. "The nausea should be fading any minute now. Stay with her. Let me know immediately when the bond progresses."

"Will do. It's good to have you back."

There was something beneath the words. An undercurrent of emotion that made me wonder if they'd been together at some point.

And that pissed me off, even though I'd never had a real claim to him. I was the one who'd told him I would find someone else to screw if he wasn't willing, after all.

In hindsight, that was probably a bad way to start a mate bond.

Then again, he was the asshole who didn't even want my name. He was definitely planning on sleeping with the woman he'd left me with. I was just going to be the token siren he used for—

I groaned, lifting my head and vomiting again.

The dizziness was only getting worse.

"It should subside soon," my mate's lover promised.

I wanted to claw her eyes out... but I didn't have claws.

Just obnoxious magic that would make her feel *better* if I used it on her.

The world spun around me violently as my nausea finally started to fade. "What's happening to me?"

"The pack's mental bond is a bitch. It's a massive, complex network. As the alpha's mate, you're at the head of it, right alongside Porter," she explained gently.

"He didn't warn me."

Not about the bite, and not about the mental bond. Not about the lover, either.

What else hadn't he said?

I missed whatever her response was, but snapped myself out of my thoughts in time to hear, "We need to get some fluids in you. The Powerade will help."

"I just need water," I said.

"I don't think you—"

"And peppermint."

"Peppermint? Why would that help?"

I ignored her question.

Apparently Porter hadn't bothered telling his lover what I was before he ditched me with her.

If I was her, I'd be *furious* to find out the guy I was sleeping with had mated to a siren. My magic would be difficult for him to resist, at the very least. It would drive him mad with lust, at the worst.

I flushed the toilet and slowly eased myself toward the bathtub off to my side. It was a shower/tub combo, and though it wasn't large, it would get the job done.

"What are you doing?" she seemed perplexed.

She knew I wasn't a wolf, but it didn't surprise me that she hadn't realized what I was. Unmated sirens were rare. She probably thought I was a vampire or something.

I turned the water on and managed to climb over the ledge of the tub. My body hit the smooth basin with a loud smack, and I used my toes to close the drain as I groaned in pain.

The water wouldn't cure me.

I would probably need to eat the crackers and drink the Powerade.

But I knew the water would give me relief from the dizziness.

"You're a *siren?*" my mate's lover demanded, as the water started covering my face.

Finally, she figured it out.

She was probably going to try to kill me for what I was while I was in the tub, but I didn't have the energy to care.

"Porter doesn't think the water can heal you," she said, her anger faded as it rose over my cheeks. "He still wants you to eat something."

I had to assume he'd communicated that to her through the mental pack bond. The one that was apparently becoming mine too.

Finally, the water covered my ears, and I had peace.

Blissful, blissful peace.

four

IZZY

TIME PASSED by painfully slow as the tub filled. Porter's lover turned the water off at some point, but I didn't acknowledge it.

Eventually, I was going to have to have an actual conversation with the woman my mate was screwing. And I was going to have to *not* try to kill her. Mostly because she had claws and teeth, and all I had was obnoxiously provocative magic.

As the minutes passed, the blissful silence I'd been looking for started to fade.

Noise began to replace it.

It was quiet at first. Like a handful of conversations running through my head.

Someone was asking someone else whether they thought Porter was going to hurt them the way Curtis had.

Another person was chasing a squirrel, their thoughts vibrant and full of adrenaline.

A group of people were arguing about what kind of magical being the alpha's new mate was, and whether I made him stronger or weaker.

It was weaker. The answer was weaker.

But I wasn't about to broadcast *that*. Everyone would find out what I was soon enough.

My entire body felt weak, but even at my strongest, I was no match for a werewolf. When I was fully fed, I was much faster than a wolf, but I was rarely fully fed.

It had been too dangerous to leave our house that frequently before we were with the vampires. Since then, I just couldn't force myself to get it on with a vamp twice a week. I'd scraped by when I had to, and thankfully only ended up being bitten by a vampire once.

Most of my sisters were more than happy to feed the vamps, but I wasn't.

Then again, a werewolf had just bitten me too. Publicly. And it hurt a hell of a lot more than a vampire's bite.

My shoulder still ached a bit, actually. It just didn't seem important given everything else I was dealing with.

The noise of the pack connection grew louder as I soaked.

Another group of wolves was prepping food for the pack. Burgers and fries. They were excited about Porter getting rid of Curtis.

A different group was carrying armloads of Curt's stuff out to a massive fire pit that looked like it had been dug there a long time ago. Rocks circled it, and it looked well-used. It was full of Curt's things, and there was another pile of them off to the side.

Someone was watching Porter growl at someone else, though they couldn't hear the conversation.

My mind brushed another wolf's, and I felt them realize I was there. They hit me with the full-force of their anger, shoving me out of their head.

I cried out in pain, reaching for the new throbbing in my temple.

The amount of effort it took was insane. I was even weaker than I realized.

A pair of hands grabbed my shoulders and lifted me out of the water. My eyes met a pair of concerned, dark orbs. Their owner was tall and built strong, her pale face framed by a sleek, dark blonde bob cut to her chin. "What happened?"

"Nothing." I tried to push her hands away so I could sink back into the tub, but she refused to let go.

"You need to eat something to regain your strength for tonight."

"What's tonight?"

Her forehead creased. "Did Porter tell you *anything*?"

Other than that he didn't plan on having sex with me?

"No."

She sighed. "Eat something, and I'll tell you."

I reluctantly sat up. My entire body shook with the effort, and I was forced to admit to myself that she was right.

I *was* too weak at the moment.

"How do you know Porter?" I should've been able to ignore their relationship, but I couldn't.

"We were close friends before... well, you know."

Before his family had been killed while he was away helping another pack, and he left the pack he was supposed to run.

"Sex close?" I was going to get *myself* killed, and I didn't even have the heart to care.

Her eyes widened. "No. Definitely not. It was three of us who were close. Me, Porter, and Evan. I'm engaged to Evan. He wears my mark around his neck. Wolves are big on public claiming, and we don't share.

So she *wasn't* screwing my mate.

That made me like her a lot more.

She set a plastic sleeve of crackers and a big bottle of Powerade on the edge of the tub. "I'm Kim. There's history between my family and Porter's. My brother was engaged to one of his sisters before everything happened. We're basically family too, now."

She waited for me to introduce myself, but I knew she'd tell Porter my name if I did.

So, I just grabbed the bottle of Powerade and forced myself to drink from it. With my nausea entirely gone, I wasn't worried about making myself sick. The illness had come with the mental connection, and I didn't think it was coming back.

Picking up on my lack of an answer, she changed gears. "What do you know about wolf shifters?"

"You turn from human to wolf. And have a mental connection, apparently."

She waited.

I pulled a few crackers from the package and bit down on one.

"That's it?"

"Yep."

She sighed heavily.

I took another bite.

Sitting down on the bathroom floor, she leaned her shoulders up against the cabinet beneath the sink. "Remember the way Porter bit you after the challenge?"

"It'd be impossible to forget the utter shock, horror, and embarrassment."

"That happens frequently around here. It's not seen as an embarrassment—it's a show of possession. Public claiming is a big thing for wolves. Evan's instincts might push him to bite me as soon as I'm with him and Porter, just to declare me his."

Some part of me still despised the sound of her with Porter, but I mentally shoved that stupidity away. My irritation was at an all-time high, considering the voices in my head.

Someone wanted to steal a pair of Curtis's shoes before the bonfire.

Another person was considering challenging Porter, but his friend was reminding him what a shit idea that was.

A group was trying to figure out the best gift for a new alpha.

"Without public claiming, the pack won't be able to acknowledge you as the alpha's mate," Kim said.

"Well, he already did that."

Her expression was hesitant enough that I knew there was more to it.

"Kim," I warned.

She grimaced. "After a mate bond is sealed, there's always a larger public claiming. During a pack run, the newly-mated couple has sex beneath a gazebo in the forest. It has curtains you can unroll for privacy—but most women just wear their mate's t-shirt to keep themselves covered while they screw."

"Tell me you're joking."

"I'm not. And there's more."

I waited.

She dragged a hand over her face. "Porter should probably be the one to explain this."

"Kim," I warned.

"Have you ever heard of a knot?"

"Pretty sure everyone knows what it means to tie a knot."

"Not that kind of knot." Her grimace deepened. "Male wolves—and wolf shifters, by extension—have a knot at the base of their erection that swells when they get off. It's wider than the rest of their cock. An unmated shifter's knot is barely noticeable, but after the bond is sealed, it gets significantly bigger. The whole point of public claiming is to prove that the man can knot his mate, and his female can take it."

"Fuck."

"Yeah."

"Does it hurt?"

"I don't know," she admitted. "But the magic it releases is so intense, you're supposed to enjoy it."

"That seems unlikely. But I don't know if Porter is even planning on doing that—so maybe I won't have to worry about it. When we sealed the bond, he made it clear he didn't want sex."

Her eyebrows shot upward. "If you don't go through with the public claiming, the pack won't recognize you as his mate. You'll be in a lot more danger. And considering you're a siren..."

"I don't need any help putting myself in danger. I'm aware."

Someone's thoughts were particularly loud as they chased someone else through the forest, and I rubbed my temple.

"Is the pack bond causing you problems?" Kim checked.

"It's just loud."

"Eating more would probably help."

I forced myself to grab another few crackers. "What are mated wolves like? Possessive, I assume?"

"Very. And despite what Porter said, I can't imagine a wolf not wanting to screw his mate. We're very physical. Wolves need to be touched, frequently. And not just sexually— though that's fun. We just hug a lot and lean on each other a lot."

"Sirens are a little like that too. One of my sisters always says that sirens require snuggles."

Her lips curved upward. "You'll fit right in, then."

"Do you guys have a pool here?"

Kim shook her head. "There's a lake out in the forest, though. It's about a mile away."

Ooh, a lake?

That was new.

I was officially itching to claim it for myself. Publicly.

It was totally too soon for that joke, but whatever.

"Perfect," I said. "How long until the bonfire?"

She went quiet for a minute, her gaze growing distant before she refocused on me. "About an hour."

"Is Porter planning on coming back to talk to me first?"

She shrugged. "I don't know for sure, but I don't think so. He killed one of Curtis's closest guys about an hour ago, and he's been interrogating a few more with Evan. You should be able to talk to him mentally now, though. The alpha can't block out his mate, and vice versa."

"How would I do that?"

"Just focus on him. The magic of the pack bond should connect you to him easily."

I focused my mind on my asshole of a mate, and sure enough, immediately felt his consciousness brush up against mine.

I flinched when I saw his fist collide with someone's face, and withdrew quickly.

"They're still interrogating," Kim said quickly.

A heartbeat later, I felt Porter's mind meet mine. *"Don't look through my eyes without warning,"* he growled at me.

"Fuck off," I snapped back. *"You haven't told me a damn thing, and I just found out we're supposed to have sex in front of your whole pack. If you didn't want me to invade your mind, you should've told me."*

"The pack won't be sitting and watching—they'll be running around."

"Not all of us have a voyeurism kink, asshole."

I felt him run a hand through his hair. It was covered in blood, and I didn't want to know why.

"If there was a way out of it, I would go with that," he finally said. *"But there's not. We'll put the curtains down."*

"If we do that, your pack will think we're wimps. And why the hell didn't you warn me about the knotting thing, either?" I shot back.

He made a noise of frustration. *"I assumed you knew basic information about wolves when you agreed to be my mate."*

"Sure you did."

He snarled into my mind. *"We're using the curtains."* Then, he ripped his consciousness away from mine.

I massaged my temple harder. "Asshole."

Kim's expression was curious. "You looked like you were fighting."

"He growled and insulted me, if that's what you're asking."

"He hasn't growled at anyone since his family was killed. He's always very... neutral. On the rare occasions we see him, at least."

Hale had said the same thing. That Porter used to be wild and fun, but had grown dark and neutral since he lost his family.

Some niggling, annoying part of me wanted to try to fix that, but I knew better. A woman couldn't fix a man. And even if she could, she shouldn't. If he deserved her, he would fix himself.

"Finish up the crackers. I'll find you something more filling to eat," Kim said, standing up. "Porter will want you in his clothes tonight, so take whatever you need from his closet. You'll be moving to Curtis's room after it's cleaned out, but this is Porter's for the moment. He hasn't been here in a long time, but even Curt knew better than to let someone else take it."

"We're sharing a room?"

She nodded. "No way around that."

I let out a breath. "Lovely."

I'd thought Blair was crazy for letting Hale force her to share a room with him, but it looked like I was about to be in the same boat.

She slipped out, leaving me alone in the bathtub, still fully clothed and absolutely soaked.

Sighing, I adjusted my position a little. My forehead creased when I felt something hard beneath my ass, and it occurred to me that I'd brought my phone.

Finally, something had worked in my favor.

I pulled the device out—it was waterproof—and dried it off on the shower curtain since there was no towel hanging nearby. With the screen dry enough, I turned it on and read the messages from my sisters.

CLEMENTINE

We love you, good luck <3

ZORA

Let us know if you need a jailbreak, we'll do our best

And by that I mean we'll ask Blair to seduce Hale into rescuing you

BLAIR

I will make that sacrifice for you ;P

But really, if he doesn't treat you right I'll find a way to get you out

I typed out a text of my own.

ME

Have you ever heard of knotting?

CLEMENTINE

Knotting what?

ME

Nvm

ZORA

Now I'm curious

AVERY

I haven't heard of it

CLEMENTINE

What is it?

ME

A wolf sex thing. Apparently I'm going to learn the details tonight

CLEMENTINE

Um, what?

I need an explanation

Stat!

AVERY

How are things with the furball?

ME

I have a weird mental bond with his pack now, and apparently he's going to screw me in the middle of the forest while other shifters are running around, so I don't know

Bad?

CLEM

HOTTT

ZORA

You have no boundaries, Clem

CLEM

I don't screw jerks. That's the boundary

ME

He didn't ask for my name, so I haven't given it to anyone. It's a whole thing. The pack is so loud in my head that I feel like I have a migraine. I think this might have been a bad call

ZORA

We all told you that

ME

Apparently I should've listened

CLEM

Nothing to do now but enjoy the ride!

Literally ;)

BLAIR

LOL

AVERY

Do you need us to find a way to get you out?

ME

The bond is permanent, so I think I'm stuck

It's too soon to call for a rescue, but I'll let you guys know if I can't handle it. I think I can make it work, though

That was total bullshit, but I couldn't ask my sisters to risk themselves to try to save me. I didn't know much about Porter, but it was clear that wolves were possessive. And he had just become the werewolf king. If the vampires tried to take me from him, it would be an act of war, and I was not going to cause a war.

I'd gotten myself into this mess.

All I could do now was make the best of it.

Or at least, try to survive.

five

IZZY

I MANAGED to get out of the tub and change into a long-sleeve t-shirt and a pair of boxers before Kim came back.

The clothes dwarfed me. Sirens didn't come in *alpha* size. Or anywhere near it. Even male sirens were significantly shorter than Porter and Damian.

I was the tallest of my sisters, but still only came in at a cool 5'6". Porter had to be at least six and a half feet tall. Maybe even taller.

But that meant I didn't have to wear pants with his shirt, so it seemed like a win to me.

I sniffed my new shirt as Kim slipped into the room with a large tray of food in her hand.

"Everything in here smells like perfume," I said.

"It's the moth balls. Porter hasn't been here in a long time." She set the food down next to me. "How many sisters do you have? You mentioned them earlier."

"I'm not supposed to talk about it." I dug my fork into the large plate of pasta. "But if I did have sisters, I would probably have four of them."

Her lips curved upward. "You're technically my alpha, so I can't break your trust without consequences. I won't tell anyone."

"Thanks. I don't know what Porter will do with the information, though."

"He won't put your family in danger. He wouldn't do that after what he's been through."

Considering what I knew about his past, and his family being slaughtered without reason, I could believe that.

"So what are the dynamics like here?" I asked her, still working on the pasta.

"That's a good question. Things were bad when Curtis was in charge. I don't know what's going to happen now. A lot will depend on how involved Porter decides to be."

"He only agreed to challenge Curtis in exchange for mating with me," I admitted. "He wanted a siren. I don't know why, because he was furious when I drank from him."

And honestly, I needed to feed on him again in the near future. Which didn't seem to bode well for me, given the way everything was going.

"At least Curt's gone," Kim said, leaning back on the bed. "We'll figure everything else out. If me and Evan have to step up, we'll do our best."

I nodded, though my true attention was fixed on the food I was just about inhaling.

She asked about my magic while I ate, and I explained everything to her. I had no reason not to. She seemed curious, and there was no way for her to use it against me. Not unless she talked Porter into refusing to drink from me. And considering his dislike, I didn't think it would take any convincing.

If he wanted me to starve, I would starve.

Which was pretty damn terrifying.

"Is there any way to quiet the pack's voices in my mind?" I asked her. "They seem to be getting louder. It's making my head hurt something fierce."

She gave me an apologetic look. "Porter's parents trained him to take over for them, so he's the only one who'll know how to answer that. The rest of us can use the pack bond, but it goes through you guys when we do. That makes it a lot louder for you."

"Great." I bit into a thick slice of garlic bread.

"At least Curtis isn't in charge anymore."

And at least Clementine wasn't at risk anymore. I sent her a quick message.

ME

Is your mate mark gone?

CLEM

Yes ma'am

My neck is freeeee

And begging to be marked by a sexy
vamp dude

ME

Don't go signing away your freedom
just yet

CLEM

I won't

You already did that enough for both of us
;)

She wasn't wrong.

As I finished eating, Kim stood up. "Evan said the bonfire's
starting. Porter's looking for you."

"He knows where to find me." I lowered myself to my back
on the bed, closing my eyes. "I could go for an early bedtime
tonight. Do you think there's any way I can convince him to
leave me alone until tomorrow?"

She laughed. "No. I'll tell him you're not leaving without
him, though."

I would rather she didn't tell him anything, but it was what
it was.

"I know you're not excited to be here, but thank you for

making that deal with him. You saved us, even if you did it unintentionally. A lot of us owe you our lives."

"The decision was purely selfish," I murmured.

"It saved us anyway. I heard a few people talking about gifts for you, so don't be surprised when they start coming in."

I did remember hearing something about a gift through the pack bond, but I'd assumed it was going to be for Porter.

"I'll be polite."

The bedroom door opened, and a grumpy, gritty voice said, "Let's go."

"You would think a woman's mate would know to ask politely if he wants to screw her in front of an audience, wouldn't you, Kim?" I drawled.

She choked out a laugh when Porter growled.

A minute later, he'd tossed me over his shoulder again and was carrying me out of the room. Kim called out a goodbye, and I waved back.

"If you carry me everywhere, people are going to think I'm with you unwillingly," I remarked. "Is that really the message you want your pack to get?"

"I don't care what message they get. There's a mark around my neck, so you were obviously willing."

I rolled my eyes. "Unless you threatened my life."

"We both know I didn't."

"They don't, though. No one's heard from you since you abandoned the pack."

"I didn't abandon them. I left, after they quietly watched their new alpha murder my mother and sisters in cold blood without intervening." His voice was flat.

The admission was so brutal, I didn't bother trying to defend them. I hadn't been there, so it wasn't like I could disagree.

"Were you in love with Kim?" I asked.

"Of course not. I barely knew her. She followed me and Evan around constantly as kids, but we were never close. Given the situation with her brother, that will never happen."

"What situation with her brother?"

His jaw tightened. "He was engaged to my sister, but didn't do a damn thing to try to protect her when she was attacked and killed. If he hadn't run away before I got back here, he would be dead already. I can feel him hiding out somewhere in the pack right now, but I can't track him through the link. I tried."

Oh, shit.

That was dark, and he was clearly still furious about it.

Time for a subject change.

"Are there any other people in the pack that I need to watch out for? Women you had relationships with?"

"No. An alpha screwing his pack is a moron looking for a challenge. Business and pleasure don't mix."

"Is our mate bond business, or pleasure?"

He didn't answer, stopping as we reached a door that led out into the forest. Silently, he set me down on my feet.

Guess he'd listened to my comment about making people think I was unwilling after all.

"Which is it?" I asked mentally, brushing my mind up against his.

The man physically shuddered. "You can't do that."

"Why not? I'm your mate, aren't I?"

He growled.

I flashed him a smile before striding through the door in front of us.

THE GATHERING WAS UTTER CHAOS.

Wolves *everywhere.*

Monstrous bonfire.

Howls and cheers with every new item of Curt's that was tossed in the fire.

I noticed a few people on the edges of the gathering, watching closely for anyone who looked angry that Curtis's things were going up in flames.

Porter led me to a seat outside the bonfire the moment we joined the group. The bastard pulled me onto his lap, his arm around my waist in an iron grip.

I didn't bother trying to get free.

Something told me it was another public claiming thing.

And as much as he was a bastard, he was a gorgeous bastard. His chest felt great against my back. His erection beneath my ass made me a little proud, too.

His nose or lips brushed my shoulder frequently. I wasn't sure whether he was doing that for show, or just because he wanted to. Maybe some of both.

We'd only been sitting down for a short while when the first shifter woman came up to me with a gift bag in her hands. She was smiling brightly, and I couldn't help but notice the thick, dark bruises around her throat.

I tried to sit up straighter, to get off Porter's lap a little, but his arm didn't budge when I pushed against it.

"Hi, Alpha," she said, her gaze fixed on me. She didn't spare a single glance for Porter. "Curtis forced me to keep his bed warm, and it was—" she choked on the words, her eyes brimming with tears and her smile faltering. "I heard from the vampires that you traded your freedom for Curtis's death. Thank you. And welcome to the Mistwood Pack." She wiped a few tears off her face and put the gift bag on my lap.

Unwilling to let her cry alone after going through what must've been literal hell, I took her hand, pulling her toward me. Kim had made it clear that wolves needed touch the way sirens did, and I never would've let my sisters go without a hug in a moment like that.

She threw her arms around me, ignoring the bastard underneath me, and I hugged her tightly. "Don't thank me. I did it for selfish reasons."

She laughed tearily. "Your selfishness saved my life, so accept the thank you."

"I guess you're welcome, then. What's your name?"

"Nora." She stepped back, staying where she was as I opened the gift.

My eyes widened "Are these gourmet chocolates?" I pulled one out, my lips parting when I saw that it was peppermint flavored. "You're my new favorite werewolf."

She smiled. "Just let me know when you run out. I have a friend with connections."

"Chocolate connections? Can I mate with you instead?" I teased.

Her teary laugh made me grin, even though the joke made Porter's arm tighten around my waist. I was literally sitting on his lap, so he could suck it up.

She squeezed my hand again before slipping away with a promise that other wolves would be bringing me gifts too, to express their thanks. Then, she rejoined a few other women nearby.

I expected to be growled at for my remark, but Porter surprised me by not saying anything.

Huh.

He even loosened his grip on my waist after she left.

A smallish man with bright red hair came up to me next, holding a gift of his own. It was in a smallish, square box that made me a little nervous. If he broke out jewelry, I was pretty sure Porter would want to kill him.

"Curtis had me locked up for refusing to join the group that attacked your sister and the vampire king," he said, and I noticed the ashen tone to his pale skin. "I would've died in prison if not for your deal. Thank you, Alpha." He handed me the box.

I gave him a quick but genuine smile as I opened the lid.

Relief washed over me when I found what looked like a large bath bomb inside.

No jewelry.

Porter's grip tightened a little more anyway.

"My sister made it with peppermint oil and leaves," he explained.

I thanked him for his thoughtfulness, and he slipped away.

Porter's grip didn't ease.

"It's just a bath bomb," I whispered.

"He was picturing you bathing with it," Porter gritted out. "Loudly. I need to claim you."

"You already did."

"I need to claim you *better*."

He was talking about sex.

I couldn't help but flush a little.

"I don't have to use it, but I'm not going to refuse a gift. Sirens are targets. The more your people like me, the more protection I'll have," I whispered.

"You don't need their protection."

"Like hell I don't. I'm mated to someone who doesn't even want to *feed* me."

His grip tightened even more. "Of course I'll feed you. I just don't want you catching me off guard with it."

"When I get hungry enough, I literally can't control it."

"I won't let you get that hungry. You need to feed twice a week, right?"

"To stay strong, yes."

"I'll put it in my calendar."

"Romantic."

"More romantic than watching me kill someone for lusting after you." He grabbed the gift box and set it down on the dirt next to our chair.

"People *are* going to lust after me, Porter. It's the nature of my power, and it's unavoidable. You're the one who wanted a siren."

"For your magic."

"That's exactly what every woman wants to hear."

Someone else came up to us with a gift, ending the conversation abruptly. Nora winked at me, and I realized they were friends.

When I unwrapped the lumpy, odd-shaped present, my eyes widened and my lips curved wickedly.

It was a vibrator.

A very large vibrator.

Porter snarled against my shoulder as the woman grinned at me. "I know arranged matings often aren't enjoyable for sirens, but I hope this makes it just a little more fun."

When she winked at me, I couldn't help but laugh.

She walked away, but I saw other people holding gifts throughout the party. It was far from over.

"I'm not waiting any longer," Porter growled, dropping that box on the ground next to the bath bomb. My chocolates went with it.

"Wait, don't—" I began, but Porter cut me off when he shifted into his wolf form as he tossed me over his shoulder yet again. I landed smoothly on his back and buried my fingers in his fur, holding on tight as he streaked into the forest.

Howls followed our departure, and he loosed one of his own. I felt his power roll through the pack's bond, and shuddered.

The man was *insanely* strong.

But the wind against my face felt amazing. I liked the feel of his body moving beneath me, too.

I lifted my head just a little. Enough that I could see the trees around us as he ran through the forest thanks to the moonlight shining through. The moon was only half-illuminated above our heads, so I didn't know how long I had until it would be full. One of the few things I did know about wolves was that the full moon affected them, somehow.

But for the moment, I focused on where I was.

On the back of a massive wolf, in the middle of a beautiful forest.

Not trapped with the vampires—not even a little.

Sure, being a part of a pack was another kind of cage. But at least it came with fresh air and trees.

Porter ran for fifteen or twenty minutes before I finally saw a rustic, wooden gazebo in front of us. There were large, rectangular cushions set up on one side of the space below it, with blankets in a basket next to them. On the other side, there was a large, comfortable-looking chair.

"No one in my family has ever taken their mate without the curtains down," he said into my mind. *"I won't be the first. I'll kill anyone who sees your pleasure."*

"Assuming this is going to be pleasurable for me?" I drawled.

His chest rumbled with humor. *"When you've climaxed on my cock, you'll realize how completely your body belongs to me."*

I couldn't help but flush a little. *"That's a bold promise when you have no idea the heights the vampires have taken me."*

"If a vampire could satisfy you, you would never have bound yourself to me. Some part of you knows you need my knot."

I heated further. *"Like hell I do."*

"We'll find out tonight, won't we?"

I gripped his fur even tighter.

"Are you on birth control?" he asked.

"Yes. I have an implant."

He growled in approval.

We reached the steps up into the gazebo, and Porter shifted back. My nails dug into his human skin as he caught my knees easily, carrying me piggy-back style and setting me on the chair.

He was bare-assed and insanely beautiful. His cock was hard, jutting out proudly, and it had good reason too.

I couldn't stop myself from staring at him as he strode

around the outside of the gazebo, untying curtains and letting the dark green fabric fall around us sheet by sheet.

I noticed a few wolves gathering around before the last curtain unrolled, cutting out the moonlight entirely and surrounding us in darkness.

"I can't see anything," I said into Porter's mind, not wanting his pack to hear me. They were supposed to think I was strong and sexy, so I didn't want them to realize I'd been blinded by their curtains.

"You don't need to see." His hands landed on my knees, and I sucked in a breath as his gorgeous, dark eyes met mine.

He was kneeling in front of me.

Hot damn.

"I'm going to taste you," he said, his voice rich and gravelly in a way that made goosebumps break out on my arms. *"And then I'm going to fuck you. When I come, my knot will tie us together. Understand?"*

"Guess I have the answer to my business or pleasure question."

He hooked his hands in the waistband of my borrowed boxers, but didn't pull them down yet. *"If you want out, this is your only chance. I won't stop after I have you on my mouth. The beast in me won't hear reason."*

"The pack won't respect me if I back out, will they?"

"No."

I let out a long breath. *"Then do your worst."*

He chuckled, and I felt like I finally got a small glimpse of the wild guy Hale had mentioned he used to be.

In one rough motion, he pulled me to the edge of the chair, tugged the boxers down my ass, and dropped the fabric on the ground.

My legs were spread wide a moment later, his nose brushing my clit as he inhaled deeply.

I saw his eyes close, just barely.

And I nearly arched myself right out of my chair when he dragged his tongue slowly over my clit without further warning.

"Fuck," I gasped, as he pinned my hips down with his hands and licked me again, slower. His mouth was so much warmer than the vampire's I'd been with last, and it had been ages since anyone screwed me before that.

The feel of his mouth on me was intense.

Intimate.

Insane.

But Porter was in absolutely no hurry at all.

I gripped the chair's armrests like they were anchoring me, struggling to breathe through the pleasure as he ate me out like I was the most delicious thing he'd ever tasted.

Like he was savoring me.

Like he didn't want it to end.

My desperation rose as he didn't pick up the pace, just licking me slowly.

The sounds I made grew louder.

Needier.

Greedier.

I tried to arch my hips, but he held me down firmly.

I grabbed his hair, but he didn't respond to my tugs and pulls on the strands.

Every time I neared my climax, he slowed even more.

When I could feel myself on the brink of pleasure, he pulled back.

"Give me your cock, now," I breathed, arching harder as I tried to take what I needed from him.

He chuckled roughly. *"You think you're ready for me?"*

"Yes."

"I'll be the judge of that." He pressed the tips of three of his fingers to my entrance, and I sucked in a breath as he sank them inside me. *"Fucking drenched for me."* There was approval in his voice, and his eyes—shit, they were hotter than anything I'd ever seen.

I tried to move against his hand, to use it the way I needed it, but he pulled out and licked his fingers clean, rumbling again.

My chest rose and fell quickly, my abdomen twisted with need.

Finally, Porter pulled me off the edge of the chair and turned me around. My ass met his bare thighs, and my lips parted when I felt the thick bulge of his cock between my legs.

My slickness coated his length, and he leaned me forward, pressing my covered tits to the chair.

His fingers brushed my clit, making me suck in a breath as he opened my thighs.

The head of his cock met my entrance—and in one rough motion, he filled me.

I cried out desperately as he stretched my body in ways I'd never imagined.

He was so much thicker than anyone else I'd ever been with.

So much.

I could barely breathe. All rational thought was so far gone, it may as well have never existed at all.

The pads of his fingers pressed against my clit as he gave me a moment to adjust. I moved my hips a little, trying to find the most comfortable position, but there wasn't one.

He was just too huge.

I panted, lingering on the edge of my orgasm. I was so close—but he wasn't giving me what I needed.

And I couldn't ask for it, because I couldn't even get my brain to work properly.

Slowly, he pulled out and sank back in.

"Your pleasure is leaking through to my side of the mate bond," he said, the words gritted out in a way that made me think he was struggling to form thoughts almost as badly as I was.

"Can't control it." I panted, my fingers digging into the chair's cushion as he pulled out and sank in deeper. Our bodies were as connected as we could possibly get.

"Feels so fucking good." The grit in in his voice, in my head, paired with the way he filled me?

It was so damn intense.

I moaned as he pulled out and drove into me again. The base of his cock started to swell, and he worked my clit harder.

The feel of his body in mine was all-encompassing.

I forgot about the gazebo.

The curtains.

The pack.

There was just Porter, and me.

And even though my feelings for him were far from pleasant, he felt absolutely incredible.

I shattered on his erection with a cry, my fingers digging deeper into the cushion as he slammed into me once, then again.

The heat of his release flooded my channel as he roared his pleasure. The base of his cock swelled bigger, and I choked out a strangled cry as the pressure of it grew otherworldly.

"You take my knot so fucking well." His teeth skimmed my sensitive shoulder, where he'd bitten me earlier. *"Tell me how it feels."*

"Unreal," I managed to get out.

Intensely erotic—and somehow, even more intimate.

He pressed my clit hard, and my hips rocked in desperation. My climax had ended, but I was so close to another one.

"The magic of our connection will drive you wild until it eases." His voice was pure gravel. *"Let it. Don't fight it. I'll feel every shred of pleasure you do while we're connected this way. Every time you climax, you'll take me with you."*

I cried out again as he eased the pressure over my clit. I moved my hips a little, desperate to chase the release I could feel building, and cried out at the light but sharp pain that answered.

"I'm going to lose my mind," I moaned aloud, unable to think clearly enough to have to conversation mentally.

"That's the point, baby. Let yourself feel it." The hand he didn't have on my clit slid under my shirt and found one of my tits, gripping hard.

"I'm not your *baby*." My nails were so deep in the cushion, it hurt. I could feel his wild, reckless magic threatening to consume me entirely, but I didn't want to give him that power over me. I wanted to stay in control. "I can't let go. I—ohh, fuck," I hissed, as he pinched my clit.

"You're close. Stop fighting it."

There was power behind his command, and I shuddered against him. With his cock buried inside me and his body wrapped around mine, I was afraid I was going to lose the battle.

"How much longer?" I gritted out.

"The first time, at least thirty minutes. Up to an hour, based on power."

Logic told me we were in for the hour.

"Surrender to my magic, Isabella."

He did know my name.

I didn't know how—but he knew.

"Your body belongs to me. Your pleasure, too. You're going to spend the next hour climaxing on my cock, so close those sexy green eyes and let go."

The command was so fierce, so hot, that I didn't even *want* to fight it.

I forced myself to back off, to stop fighting the sensations I was feeling. To let out a slow breath and let myself sink into the pleasure he was offering me.

And slowly, the untamed magic within him took over entirely.

I screamed with pleasure at the first, heightened climax as my body squeezed his knot.

Porter swore and snarled filthy things into my ear as he filled me with his release again. His power pushed me higher before I came down from the high.

He worked my clit, and I pushed back on his cock, forcing his knot deeper into me and shattering my control again.

And again.

And again.

The orgasms were incomparable to anything I had ever experienced before—and Porter's repeated declarations about me being his only made the releases even more intense.

When his knot finally started to soften, I was soaked with sweat, and sticky with both of our releases. The insides of my legs and my entire ass were drenched, and the whole gazebo smelled of me and Porter.

Shock, heat, and exhaustion set in as I finally started to catch my breath.

"The pack will have no doubt that you're mine." Porter's voice held carnal satisfaction that made goosebumps break out on my skin.

"I don't even want to think about what they just heard. Who told you my name?"

"I asked Hale before I met you." He slowly slid his hand down from my breast. It moved over the curve of my waist and around my ass, before he dragged his fingers over the place we were connected. My skin was hot and tender, but his touch was gentle enough that it felt good.

"That was..." I trailed off, not sure what to say.

Honestly, I was starving again. Both for emotions and real food.

But I wasn't sure when Porter would be willing to let me feed on him again, after the drama of the last time.

So, that was a little scary.

He slid his finger deeper inside me, testing the space between my knot and his walls. He was just trying to see if he was soft enough to pull out, but his cock throbbed inside me anyway.

"How can you still be horny? My vagina is going to be sore for days."

"Our magic will help you recover much faster than that. And I'm not horny. It's just a fucking turn-on to own you like this."

"I noticed."

He chuckled.

"I'm not going to heal if you don't let me feed on you, though," I added, and his humor disappeared. *"Your pack link's magic seems to have drained mine."*

"Fine. Do it before my knot is gone so I can fight it."

Well, that was rude.

Most people would be *thrilled* to feel siren magic, and he wanted to fight it?

I turned my head to the side, and he leaned forward, kissing me lightly.

I buried a hand in his hair, pulling him a little closer, and put my tongue in his mouth as I tapped into my magic.

His emotions hit me like a freight train.

Pure, unbridled lust.

Endless desire.

Fierce need.

Those more surface-level feelings were gone quickly, though, replaced by the same dark feast I'd tasted on him earlier.

Self-hatred.

Fear.

Despair.

Loss.

Grief.

Guilt.

I wasn't entirely sated when he ripped his mouth from mine, but I was getting there. And I'd been expecting him to pull away, that time.

He eased his knot out of me, and my entire body seemed to groan at the loss. With his expression dark, he grabbed the boxers I'd borrowed off the floor and put them in my arms, then stood up and strode out of the gazebo without looking back, leaving me in complete and utter darkness.

The curtains fell smoothly into place, and I lowered my forehead to the chair's cushion, taking a deep, shaky breath in.

Howls rang through the forest around me.

Being mated to a werewolf was wild. Absolutely, insanely wild.

But I was starting to think I might be a huge fan.

I gave myself a minute to catch my breath, then finally stood up. My legs were shaky, and I was sore between my thighs, but I felt good.

Really good.

I slipped the boxers on even though the last thing I wanted to do was soak them with Porter's release. And there was a *lot* of it, so there was no way around that.

As unpleasant as it was to feel his pleasure dripping down the insides of my thighs, there was some amount of pride, too.

We were permanently mated—and I could obviously please him. That felt good.

I slipped out of the gazebo a minute later, moving through the curtains like Porter had.

There was a wolf sitting at the bottom of the steps that led up to the structure, which caught me off-guard. It was so dark that I couldn't make out the fur color, and could barely tell what size it was. It seemed a lot smaller than Porter, but I couldn't be sure.

A mind brushed against mine through the pack's bond, and it felt like a request. I let it in, and realized it was Kim.

"Porter asked me to take you back to the Manor," she said into my mind.

So she was the wolf in front of me.

"It's weird that he ditched me here after screwing me, don't you think?" I asked, stepping closer to her.

Her humor curled through my mind. *"Wolves are always very snuggly after sex, so yes."*

"I don't know if he qualifies as a normal wolf, given the situation."

"He's watching us closely from the trees, so I think he's feeling the normal things. He's just fighting it."

"Lovely."

The wolf made a sound that reminded me of a laugh, and my lips curved upward.

"I'm not getting on your back while I'm covered in his release. That's disgusting," I said, sitting down on the bottom step of the gazebo. Not only was it gross, but I was possessive enough not to want anyone else smelling like his pleasure.

Wolves had an amazing sense of smell—every other wolf in the pack would notice his scent on whoever carried me.

"I'll take a dip in the lake afterward to erase the smell. Evan is off doing something for Porter, so he won't care."

"Thanks for the offer, but I'll wait for him to get angry enough to carry me back himself."

"Of course." There was something in her tone that I didn't understand. Disappointment, or annoyance? Maybe she was just worried Porter would be angry with her.

She took off into the trees, and I scanned the dark forest around us, looking for Porter's dark eyes. There were at least a dozen wolves around, but I couldn't tell which was my mate.

I reached for Porter through the pack's link. *"I'm not letting anyone else carry me back. You have five minutes to take me yourself, or I'll walk back alone. My feet will end up bloody and I'll probably get myself lost if I try, but I'm proud enough to do it anyway."*

He growled into my mind, but a moment later, he was storming up to the steps. He looked even bigger after I'd seen how small Kim was.

When he lowered himself to the ground, I slid onto his back again.

We were both quiet as he slipped through the trees, headed back to the Manor. It wasn't until he ditched me in his room that I finally spoke into his mind again.

"If you ever screw anyone but me, I'll kill you."

He snapped invisible teeth at me. *"If another man ever touches you, I'll dismember him and lock you in my room."*

"Glad that's settled."

He tried to shut me out of his mind. Though the bond didn't allow that, I withdrew anyway. The bastard could have his privacy.

six

IZZY

I TOOK a long bath before curling up in bed. I'd locked the door, but assumed that Porter had a key and could get in easily enough.

My sisters had texted me again, but I didn't answer them.

There wasn't much to say.

I'd screwed my mate, and it was amazing, but he was still an angry bastard who I genuinely didn't want to share my life with. Period.

So, I just closed my eyes and let myself drift off. Like all parasitic magical beings, I couldn't sleep well without a coffin of sorts to make me feel safe. We called them canopy beds, with a lid of sorts that could raise and lower to let us in and out.

But, I would try to sleep anyway.

. . .

AFTER TOSSING and turning all night, I finally gave up on sleep around 5 AM. The sun wasn't up yet, and wouldn't be for a while.

And my mate?

He hadn't come to bed.

I had no idea where he'd been, who he'd been with, or what he'd been doing. All night.

Which was just *fantastic*.

Our traded threats the night before were far from a guarantee that he wasn't actually going to cheat on me, so that didn't feel great.

I ran a hand over my face and grabbed my phone off the side table. The battery was lingering at a solid 17%, so it still had a little juice left.

There were a bunch more texts from my sisters, and a few missed calls.

Though Avery was the one I usually turned to when I needed to talk, I hit the button to call Blair back. She was the only one with a mate, which made her much easier to talk to about this shit.

She answered immediately. "Hey, Iz. Are you okay?"

"I think so." I sat up, making myself comfortable with a few pillows behind my back, and tugged my fingers through my hair. When they caught on the knots, I winced.

I should've brushed it out after my bath the night before, but laziness had prevailed. And tossing and turning hadn't helped anything.

After a beat of hesitation, I blurted the question on my mind. "Don't men usually want to sleep with their mates? Not just for the sex—but for the actual sleeping? Wasn't that a big deal for Hale?"

"Yeah, he won't sleep without me," she agreed. "I don't know if it applies to all mated men. Want me to ask him?"

"I don't know. Maybe?"

"Maybe, or yes?"

"Yes," I admitted reluctantly. "I'm kind of scared Porter's going to cheat on me or something. He said he won't, but..."

"But you don't trust him."

"No."

"You just met him, and you don't know him. I think not trusting him is fair. He'll have to earn your trust if he wants it."

Her words eased some of the tension in my shoulders. "Yeah, you're right."

"Okay, I just got to the office. Let me ask Damian about the sleep thing and I'll call you back."

"Alright. Thanks."

"Of course." She hung up, and I dropped the back of my head against the wood behind me.

Closing my eyes, I let out a long breath.

The pack's voices were still running through my head, but they were a little quieter and more subdued.

A kid was playing tag with a bunch of other little wolves.

Someone was washing their hair, singing along passionately to a pop song that played.

As small group of men and women were gathered together, arguing about whether or not I was a suitable mate for their new alpha and if the pack would be better off with me dead.

That last one had me jerking upright, my eyes widening.

I tried to focus on that person, but my phone rang again, distracting me. The distraction pulled me too far, and I couldn't find them again.

Letting out a soft groan, I answered my phone.

Suddenly, whether or not Porter wanted to sleep with me didn't seem to matter.

"Hey," I said.

"Hey. Damian says it's a security thing, and nearly all mated men should feel the same way about it. It's pretty much impossible for a guy to sleep without his mate next to him after he's bound to her. I didn't tell him that you asked, by the way—just in case you wanted to keep it a secret. If he asks, I don't want to lie to him, though."

"It's fine, you can tell him." I tugged my fingers through my hair again, still wincing. "So you think if a mated guy didn't sleep by his mate, he didn't sleep at all?"

"Probably not," she agreed.

Damn.

I reached out to Porter's mind, trying to do so carefully so he wouldn't feel my intrusion.

He was focused on the forest around him; he was running.

Had he been running all night?

He couldn't have, could he?

I'd have to pay attention if he didn't sleep next to me again the next time I went to bed.

"Do you want to talk about what happened?" Blair checked.

"I don't know." I closed my eyes. "Apparently, wolves screw their mates in public to claim them."

Blair sucked in a breath.

"Yeah. There's this gazebo in the forest. He closed the curtains over it, so no one could see us, but I'm sure they could hear."

"Holy shit. Did he force you?"

I laughed softly. "No. He wouldn't. I don't think so, at least. He definitely didn't have to. It was fucking incredible. Mated wolf sex is *not* like normal siren sex."

"But he didn't sleep with you afterward?"

"No." I bit my lip. "He carried me back to the Manor and left. I haven't seen him since."

"Wow."

"Yeah. I don't know what to do, now. Or what to think. Or even how to feel. I usually have an idea, but I'm freaking clueless. What's my next move here?"

"Well, what's the pack like?"

"Some of them love me. They gave me presents. Chocolate, a bath bomb, and a vibrator."

Blair snorted. "So it's heaven."

"Right?" My lips curved upward just a little, but my smile faded. "I think some of them want me dead, too."

"Well, that's not good."

"Nope."

"Do they respect or fear Porter enough not to try to hurt you? Is he doing anything to try to get them under control?"

"I have no idea."

"Then I think that's your next move. Figure out the situation. Learn how much of the pack wants you dead, and how much of it loves you. Decide whether or not Porter can remove that risk."

"Okay, I can do that." I'd need to focus on the pack bond. If I spent enough time submerged in it, I could decide where to go from there. "If he can't remove the risk..."

"Then you leave," Blair said simply. "Not everyone at Vamp Manor *likes* sirens, but they fear or respect Damian enough that we're safe here. If Porter can't make that happen for you, you'll come back. If he tries to keep you there, we'll break you out."

"Thank you."

"I'm your sister. No thanks required. Do they have a pool there?"

"No, but there's a lake."

"Oooh. I want a lake."

"I'm sure if you tell Hale, he'll figure out a way to make you one."

Blair laughed. "Or he'll just fuck me in the pool until I decide I'm fine without it."

I snorted. "TMI."

Despite my remark, I couldn't hide my smile. It was good to hear her happy. She'd struggled with feeding our entire lives, so I was glad she was finally healthy, happy, and safe.

"Sorry! Love you. Call me soon, okay?"

"Alright. Love you too. Bye."

I hung up, dropping my phone on my bed and forming a plan in my mind.

I gave myself two more minutes to stay in bed before I forced myself to get up and moving.

There was shit to do.

AN HOUR LATER, I'd grabbed a plate of food from the buffet-style cafeteria the pack ran, accepted a few more presents (many of which were sex toys), retrieved the gifts from the night before, dropped all of said presents back in my room, and finally headed out on my way to the lake.

Despite my uncertainty about my mating situation, the people in the pack who did seem to like me *really* liked me. Which was nice. I definitely couldn't complain.

Thanks to them, I had a hand-drawn map to the lake. And a basket of snacks to leave next to the water, in case I decided to make my swim a long one. And a stack of towels. And a brush, plus a bunch of hair ties.

All of that, on top of a dozen vibrators and dildos. Porter would've been pissed, but he would've had to actually be there to care.

A guy I'd met in the cafeteria had even offered to French-braid my hair. I usually had to ask Zora or Clem to do it when I wanted it done, so I accepted without hesitation. It was a little uncomfortable to have some random man's hands in my hair, but absolutely worth making my day easier by getting my hair out of my face.

I headed out and walked down the paved path like I'd been instructed. My basket of snacks was hanging from my elbow, and my towel was draped over my shoulder. My hair was tied back in two surprisingly-perfect French braids, and all I had on was the same black, sporty bikini I'd been wearing the day before.

When I reached a branch in the road, I paused and squinted down at the napkin that held my map, trying to decide which way to go.

Considering I'd spent most of my life hiding from magical beings who'd want to use me for my magic, I was a shitty navigator.

A shadow caught my attention as it stretched over me a minute later, and I looked over to see who it belonged to.

When I saw a tall, blond guy who looked kind of like Curtis had, my stomach clenched. There was a band around his throat that marked him as mated, but that didn't mean he wasn't part of the group that wanted me dead.

He grinned. "Hey, I'm Evan."

Oh.

It was Kim's fiancé. One of Porter's closest friends.

On second glance, the mark on his neck was the dark blue of an unsealed bond.

"Hi," I said. There was no point in keeping my name a secret anymore, since Porter clearly knew it. "I'm Izzy."

He sniffed the air. "Why do you smell like Arthur Long?"

"Some guy braided my hair for me. His name might've been Arthur. There were so many people, their names went in one ear and out the other."

"Porter's not going to like that," Evan warned, stepping up closer to me and sniffing the air above me. His lips twisted in a grimace. "*Definitely* not going to like that."

"Porter's been out all night doing who knows what with who knows who, so he doesn't get a say."

Evan snagged the napkin from my fingers, and I bit back a huff. "Trying to find the lake?"

"Yeah. I'm shit with maps."

"Whoever drew this forgot to include this intersection. Left takes you toward the other entrances into Wolf Manor. Right takes you to the sidewalk that wraps around the other wings too. Straight takes you down the forested path that connects our chunk of the forest to the expanse of it around Mistwood, so it's the default choice for a wolf."

"Maybe I'm not as bad with maps as I thought."

"Only time will tell. Do you have a pen?"

I dug through my snack basket, handing it over when I found one.

The people who loved me were prepared for anything.

I kinda loved them too.

He held the napkin against his palm as he added a few more roads to it, along with labels as to where they went. When he handed it back, I snapped a picture with my phone, then stuck it back in the basket.

"Thanks," I said, heading straight again.

I expected Evan to walk the other way, but he kept pace with me. Considering his long-ass legs, it wasn't difficult for him.

"You should have someone with you all of the time until we get the pack settled. We're still making our way through the people who were loyal to Curtis. Some of them who aren't willing to follow Porter are being removed from the pack, and killed if they pose a threat," Evan said. "I thought Kim was putting together your bodyguard rotation. She must've forgotten."

"Is Porter helping with that? Last I checked, he was in the forest."

"His help isn't necessary at this point."

"If some of Hale's vampires were working against him, he would personally hunt them down and kill them," I said matter-of-factly.

I may not have liked living with the vampires, but I paid attention. Hale was directly involved in everything that mattered. If Blair had been at risk, she wouldn't have left his side.

That obviously wasn't the case with Porter and me.

"The pack is a family," Evan said. "We trust each other to take care of business. Porter trusts us."

"He doesn't want to be involved, does he?"

Evan let out a slow breath. "Not particularly."

Yeah.

That was what I thought.

"We both know he's only here because he wanted a siren mate—even if I'm not sure why he did. Can the pack ever be safe if the alpha doesn't actually want to run it?" I asked bluntly.

"Considering our situation before he came here, it's already significantly safer. Even if he leaves us to do everything else, we're not being controlled by a dictator anymore, and no one can take him down in a challenge. That's good enough for us."

"Is it?"

"Yes."

I didn't reply to that.

It didn't sound good enough to me.

"Why do *you* think he wanted to mate with a siren?" I asked Evan, when he still didn't leave.

"I probably shouldn't say," he said.

"Then I probably shouldn't stay here," I tossed back, my anger flaring. "My *mate* is off somewhere in the forest while people in his pack are trying to decide if and how they should kill me. Does that sound like a safe situation to be in? I agreed to mate with him—I didn't agree to sacrifice my life because he's too fucking lazy to get his pack in order."

"It's not *laziness*. Porter has been in a very dark place ever since he lost his family. If he could pull himself out of it, he would, but he can't. Honestly, I think he mated with you because he thinks it's his only shot at making his way back to who he used to be."

"Then why isn't he with me?"

"I imagine coming back from hell hurts."

"Then he needs to rip off the band-aid and get it over with."

Evan snorted. "If he was himself, he'd be fucking obsessed with you."

"Considering I slept alone last night, that clearly isn't the case."

Evan nodded. "You want to know what I think?"

"Enlighten me," I drawled.

He flashed me another, smaller grin. "I think he needs a distraction. And you're the perfect solution."

"I'm his *mate*, not his *distraction*."

"Right. And there's one easy way to distract a mated man."

We continued walking.

I wasn't sure I liked Evan. He definitely seemed to be on Porter's side, not mine.

"I am *not* going to try to seduce him. He ditched me right after he screwed me in front of his pack," I reminded him.

"Not his best move, but hear me out. I'm not talking about seduction—I'm talking about jealousy."

My forehead creased. "How am I going to make him jealous? He's nowhere near me, and he knows I'm his."

"The pack link. I'll mention Arthur doing your hair. It'll piss him off, and he'll come running back. When he gets here, he'll smell Arthur in your hair, and he won't let you out of his sight for a while. As soon as he tries to leave, we'll figure out another way to make him jealous, to drag him back."

"That sounds like a good way to get Arthur murdered."

Evan grinned. "I'll tell him what's going on and hide him away until Porter's anger has died down. He'll be on board with it. This is going to be perfect."

"I'm headed out for a swim. If Porter doesn't find me before I get in the water, it's going to be too late. I'm not waiting around for that asshole."

"He'll beat you to the lake," Evan said without hesitation. "You've got a thirty-minute walk, and he'll be racing back here like hell is on his heels."

"We'll see," I said, continuing forward as Evan stayed back.

"Just follow the map, and you'll find it easily. I have work to do, so I'll send someone I trust to follow you for your protection. Tell me what happens when he catches you."

"I don't have your phone number," I called over my shoulder, when he started jogging away.

"Use the pack link!"

Right.

The pack link.

I reached out to Evan mentally, and found him with ease. *"If this blows up in my face, I'm blaming you."*

He chuckled. *"Go ahead. Porter's lost too many people to kill me."*

The words made my throat swell, but I forced myself to keep walking.

Losing people hurt like hell, but it wasn't an excuse for the way my mate had treated me. So, I wasn't going to excuse him for it. No matter how jealous Evan made him.

seven

PORTER

I WAS FUCKING DROWNING in my thoughts.

I didn't deserve a mate.

I didn't deserve a siren.

I didn't deserve *Izzy*.

And yet I wanted her so violently, it was all I could do to keep breathing.

My emotions warred.

Lust and loss.

Possessiveness and guilt.

Devotion and self-hatred.

Her magic had given me the only light I'd seen in what felt like a lifetime, but it burned so badly that I wasn't sure I'd be able to withstand it again the next time she needed to feed.

Evan's mind brushed mine, and I reluctantly let him in. After so many years without a pack bond, the connection was a bitch.

But at the same time, it felt *right* in a way I didn't have words to describe.

"Hey, man. I ran into your female on her way to the lake, and I think I smelled Arthur's scent in her hair. Not sure what's going on, but you might want to look into it," Evan said, his voice just as upbeat as always.

I skidded to a stop, growling, *"Arthur Long?"*

"Yeah. It's probably nothing," he added quickly. *"A bunch of the pack was fawning over her in the cafeteria, so he probably just bumped into her or something."*

"I'll handle it," I snarled.

If my mate had Arthur Long's scent in her hair, he was going to die.

CLEM

I guess I'll just have to keep screwing gorgeous, delicious vampires

Sigh

ZORA

Woe is you

CLEM

Woe is us

I have slept with unmated wolves, though, and that's still amazing

BLAIR

Personally, I don't think it gets better than vampires ;)

ME

You have no choice but to say that

If you agreed that mated wolf sex was better, Hale would probably kill someone

ZORA

Or many someones

BLAIR

He's not THAT volatile

He'd probably just screw me until I took it back

And I would take it back, because I'm right about the vamp stuff :P

CLEM

Your bias is showing

But it's adorable, so I'm here for it

ZORA

You share the same bias, too

 eight

IZZY

EVAN'S MAP was actually really easy to follow, so I texted my sisters back to give them a summary of the screwing, knotting, and being ditched that had happened the night before while I walked.

Their responses had me fighting a grin.

CLEM

I WANT TO FUCK A WOLF

AVERY DOES TOO, SHE'S JUST TOO EMBARRASSED TO ADMIT IT

ZORA

You would have to mate him to get the perks you're looking for, and it doesn't sound like Izzy recommends it

ME

I don't

CLEM

This is true

"Who the fuck are you texting?" a gorgeous, gravelly voice demanded just before my phone was plucked out of my arms.

The scent of him alone told me who it was before I looked over and saw him. Yeah, he was naked. Like usual. It was annoying, in a way that made me want to sit on his cock. "It's my sisters, Porter."

He scrolled through the last handful of texts, and though my face warmed, his shoulders relaxed. He handed the device back, and I tucked it in my snack basket.

Stepping closer, he stopped me with an arm in front of my chest.

Then, he leaned over and sniffed my hair.

A savage growl tore through him, and I nearly shivered. He dropped his arm and started to turn, and my gut told me he was going to hunt Arthur down and kill the bastard.

I stepped between him and the Manor, deciding to go with playing dumb. "What are you freaking out about?"

"Arthur had his hands in your hair," Porter snarled. "He needs to die."

"He braided my hair for me. I don't know how to do it myself," I said. "If you kill him for that, I'm going back to the vampires."

"Go ahead and try. My wolves have orders not to let you leave."

"You're trapping me here?" I raised my voice, anger rising with it.

"Of course I am. You're my mate, and my alpha female. You're safe here."

"How can I be safe surrounded by wolves who want me dead, Porter?" I stepped away. "Go ahead and kill Arthur. I don't care. I'll find someone else to braid my hair tomorrow. Maybe someone who'll actually spend the night with me instead of leaving me to sleep alone after screwing me in front of his pack."

Porter roared, and I resumed my walk to the lake without looking back at him.

Part of me expected him to catch me, or stop me, but he didn't. I heard his paws on the dirt a moment later, and knew he was leaving me.

Again.

I reached out mentally to Evan. *"He was just here. He's pissed. The plan failed, so I hope you hid Arthur really well."*

"We're good, Porter won't find him. And when he can't get to Arthur, his instincts will drive him back to you."

"Sure they will."

"They will. Trust me."

"I've known you for less than an hour."

"Trust the process, then."

"Alright." I grabbed a candy bar out of my snack basket. Sugar therapy was definitely needed after this conversation. *"I'll be under the water when you need me. Cross your fingers that the lake is too deep for Porter to reach me."*

"It's not, but the water is too murky. He won't find you."

"That works too. Thanks."

"Good luck."

The conversation ended, and I kept walking.

Less than five minutes later, I finally reached the lake.

Somehow, it was even better than I'd hoped.

It stretched further than I could see, with a boat dock a few yards to my left and a single, small boat tied to it. It was a boating-sized lake, so I couldn't believe there weren't any wakeboarding or surfing boats out there. It was September, so the water was a little cold for anyone who wasn't a siren, but not *that* cold.

And with the forest tucked around it and gorgeous rocks surrounding it, it looked like a natural sanctuary.

Yeah, the water was pretty filthy, but my magic would make it clear and blue over time. If I could get a few of my sisters out to swim with me, we could take care of that even faster.

I snapped a picture and sent it to them, along with a message.

ME

So there are two perks to being mated to a wolf

But I might need some help cleaning the water

CLEM

I'M ON MY WAY

AVERY

Same

ZORA

I'll text security to get us protection

Let's do this

BLAIR

Ooooh, I want in too

I can arrange a particularly strong vampire bodyguard ;)

AVERY

Wait

Isn't the wolf pack trying to kill you?

ME

Some of them. Theoretically. I don't have concrete evidence.

Just nearly concrete evidence.

ZORA

We probably shouldn't risk it

CLEM

What point is there to living if we can't swim in gorgeous lakes?

ZORA

Now you're just being dramatic

BLAIR

I'll figure out if there's a way we can do it safely

Give me a few hours to talk to Damian

ME

No rush

The longer you wait, the more stable the pack will be

In theory

ZORA

Well that's convincing

ME

Believe me, I know

Gotta go!

I dropped my phone back in the snack basket and set it up under a tree. My towels joined it. After a moment of hesitation, I let a wicked grin stretch across my face and stripped out of my bikini too.

Porter was going to be pissed, but I didn't care. If he was allowed to walk around naked after shifting all the time, I was allowed to swim in the nude.

It was good to be free, even if it came with a few shitty consequences.

I was going to miss my sisters fiercely if they couldn't leave Vamp Manor. Especially if my asshole of a mate wouldn't let me leave the wolf wing. Sirens need each other.

Wading into the water, I sighed at the feel of it. Where I touched it, I could already see the water growing clearer.

Yeah, the wolves' lake was *mine*.

I COULDN'T HAVE BEEN underwater for more than an hour when I heard from Porter again. I spent all of my time down there lost in the pack bond, trying to figure out exactly how many people wanted me dead.

I didn't have a solid number, but there were at least a few. I wasn't good enough at navigating it to figure out who they were, exactly, but I hoped I'd get there.

It was an imperfect process. And an imprecise one.

But hey, at least I knew there were people who wanted me dead. And I was getting a little better and working the pack's link, which seemed like a success.

"Where are you, and why is your bikini by a tree?" Somehow, Porter sounded even angrier than he'd been before.

I would make sure to thank Evan for that.

I sent him a mental image of the dark, murky lake, with fish swimming around me.

"You're alone?" he demanded.

"Do you have anyone else in your pack who can breathe underwater?"

His responding scoff made me snort. *"You should be wearing your swimsuit."*

"You should be wearing your clothes every time you shift out of your wolf form, but you don't see me commanding you to get dressed."

"Your body is mine," he snapped.

"And yours isn't mine?"

I felt more than heard his huff of anger. *"Did you warn Arthur that I was coming for him?"*

"No. I don't even remember what he looks like. I don't think I could find him in the pack link if I tried."

"Try."

I focused on the vague memory I had of Arthur, but I genuinely didn't remember anything about him except his dark hair. And even that had only reminded me of Avery's, so it made me think of her, not him. *"It didn't work,"* I said.

"So he knew I'd smell him on your hair, and hid from me," Porter growled.

"I don't know why you're so mad about this. You're keeping me away from my sisters, who usually braid my hair. He offered, and I took him up on it. It's no different than accepting gifts from the rest of your pack."

"Do you want any of my she-wolves running their hands through my hair?" he demanded.

My stomach clenched, even with the water easing my stress. *"That's beside the point. I'm not the one who abandoned you after fucking you while the whole pack listened in. Or left you to sleep alone, without knowing where I was or who I was with."*

"I needed time to think," he gritted out.

"And I needed to not feel used, but somehow, your needs superseded mine."

"That's not what we're discussing. You let another man put his hands in your hair."

"For all I knew, you could've been putting your cock in another woman while I tossed and turned in your bed."

"You could've looked into my mind at any moment to know that wasn't true."

"I shouldn't have to check on my mate to make sure he's not cheating on me in the middle of the night," I snapped back.

"I shouldn't have to wonder what else my mate did with one of my wolves while he braided her hair."

I glowered at a massive fish that swam lazily past me. *"Sealing the mate bond was obviously a mistake."*

"Apparently," he growled. "Get out of the water. I need to see you."

"Kiss my ass, Furball. I'm not getting out. Good luck finding me."

He snarled into my mind, and I tried to push him out, focusing on the rest of the pack bond again.

. . .

I WANTED to get out and eat a snack a few hours later, but Porter was still growling and snapping at me. That made me pretty sure he was waiting for me outside the lake.

Leaving would mean letting him catch me.

The bastard could lock me in his room or something.

So, I stayed under the water.

I swam close to the surface to check the time every now and then. When the sun was up high in the sky, I knew it was around noon. When it was lower, I'd made it to the late afternoon. And when I finally looked into the sky and saw the moon shining, I knew I'd won our little fight.

Porter was even more pissed than he had been earlier, but I didn't care. He could be as angry as he wanted. He'd treated me like shit, and I wasn't letting that go.

There were dozens of wolves around when I emerged from the water. I ignored their gazes—and the snarl of my alpha —as I strode toward the tree where I'd left my things.

Of course, Porter was waiting there.

With his gigantic biceps bulging, his cut abdomen tensed, and his eyes flooded with fury.

He was already walking toward me with a bundle of fabric in his hand—and he was wearing shorts.

He reached me long before I got back to my clothes, and unceremoniously yanked the fabric he was holding over my head. It seemed to be one of his t-shirts. The one he wasn't wearing, maybe.

When I didn't stick my hands through the armholes right away, he fished them out and tugged them through.

Then, he leveled his furious gaze with mine.

I pushed past him as our minds collided so he could snarl at me again, but I ignored his anger.

Porter grabbed my towel and basket of snacks before I could. He draped the towel over my shoulders as he walked beside me, not seeming to care that I was ignoring him. When he inhaled against my hair again, he grunted in what actually sounded like relief.

Then, he dragged me to his chest.

And he hugged me.

I didn't hug him back.

That bastard was going to have to grovel if he wanted to earn that from me.

"I'll wear pants. No more swimming naked," he said into my mind, the words clearly a command.

"You are *not* my alpha," I said aloud.

Someone nearby gasped, and I immediately regretted the comment.

If that got me killed, there would be no one to blame but me.

Porter's arms tightened around me just before he lifted me off the dirt and carried me into the trees, away from the lake and the wolves around it. When we were out of sight, he set me down long enough to strip out of his shorts. He tossed them into the basket before shifting forms, then gestured for me to get on his back.

I scowled, and didn't move.

"We obviously have things to talk about. I'll carry you to our room, and we'll figure it out," he said into my mind.

"You're assuming I want to figure things out with you. I don't."

"We're mated. You can talk to me now, or you can deal with me following you like a storm cloud until you finally give in."

"Bastard," I bit out.

"Just get on my back."

As much as I didn't want to let him have his way, it would be a nightmare to walk all the way back to the Manor with a wolf tailing me. And growling at me.

So, with a sound of annoyance, I threw a leg over his back and climbed on. I gripped his fur tighter than I needed to, but he didn't complain.

Porter grabbed the basket in his mouth—which made me bite back a snort—and took off.

We made it back to the Manor *much* faster than I would've on foot, which I couldn't deny was nice. He stayed in his wolf form as we approached the automatic doors, and carried me down a different hallway than the one I'd usually gone through.

"Where are you going? Our room is the other way."

"The pack finished cleaning out the alpha's quarters a few hours ago. Our things have been moved in already."

Oh, geez.

I was going to have to adjust to yet another room.

Would I ever feel at home outside the water again?

I wondered if Porter's family had lived in the alpha's quarters, but didn't ask. Considering how much he was already struggling with his past, I didn't want to remind him. I didn't particularly like the guy, but I did have a heart.

I reached out to open the door from Porter's back, and when he stepped into the room, I let out a breath I hadn't realized I was holding.

The room was cozy, with sage green walls, and the same rustic-looking flooring as the rest of Wolf Manor. The walls were full of framed family photos.

My heart squeezed for the man who'd lost the people he obviously loved so fiercely.

I didn't want to hurt him, but I would be extremely uncomfortable living in a place that was basically a shrine to his loved ones. A few pictures would be great, but on every single wall, in every single photo?

That wasn't going to work for me.

"My moving truck arrived today," Porter said into my mind. *"Everything is mine. Nothing in here should smell like Curtis."*

That was more important to him than me, I thought, but didn't say aloud.

He set me on my feet and shifted back before making his way around the room to check everything out.

"I'm going to shower," I said, needing some breathing room to figure out how to approach the décor conversation. "My new lake is filthy."

"As opposed to most lakes?"

"Siren magic purifies water. I'll eventually make my lake cleaner than any bathtub. It's going to take a while without my sisters, but it'll get there."

"Why can't your sisters come?"

"There are too many people here who want me dead, and even more people who would want an unmated siren for themselves. We're not in the habit of risking our lives unnecessarily, so they're staying where they're safe." I stepped through the doorway into the bathroom. There was no door to close, just a curtain that had been pulled to the side, so there was no privacy at the moment.

"I could keep your sisters safe for as long as they wanted to stay," Porter growled into my mind, because of the physical distance between us. *"I wouldn't let anything happen to them."*

My gaze collided with a picture of Porter carrying one of his younger sisters on his back, and another one in his arms.

It occurred to me that this might be a touchy subject for him. Being able to protect sisters.

My sisters weren't his, but... well, we were mates. If I told him I didn't think he could protect them, that would hurt him. More than I could possibly understand, probably.

"I believe you," I said simply. It wasn't a lie. I'd seen Porter fight, and I believed that if he decided to, he could keep them safe. *"But you'd have to arrange it with Hale. Vampires would have to come too. My sisters don't trust easily, and Hale has basically become a brother to them. Not to mention, he wouldn't let Blair come here without him."*

"Do you trust easily?"

I smiled a bit sadly, and didn't answer him.

I trusted people less than any of them, except Zora.

The bathroom was gorgeous, with a large soaking tub and a walk-in shower with glass walls. I stripped my clothes off and slipped into the shower, turning it on and letting out a sigh as the water fell over me.

I felt eyes on me, but didn't turn around. If Porter wanted to stare, he could. We *were* mates. I didn't know if I'd let him touch me after he'd growled at me so much, but there was no point in asking him not to look.

"I can't stop thinking about the way you took my knot," he said.

Apparently *he* hadn't noticed the pictures of his sisters staring at us.

"If you want to screw again, you can just say that," I said, still not turning around. "No need to beat around the bush."

"Alright, fine. I want to fuck you again."

"I'm not doing it unless you agree to let me feed from you whenever I want."

There was a moment of silence.

A long moment.

"I can't do that," Porter finally said, his voice rough.

"Why not?"

"Your magic is... too much."

I scowled. "You're the one who wanted to mate with a siren. You don't get to hate my magic."

"Not *too much* in a bad way."

"*Too much* is an insult, Porter.

"It's not an insult. If something is *too much* for me, I can't handle it. That implies that there's something wrong with me, not you."

"That's bullshit. Me being too much implies that I'm the one who was built wrong, and it's not true. Any other wolf in this pack would be thrilled to feel my magic while I feed on them. I—"

"You're perfect." His hands landed on my bare hips, and my eyes closed.

Why did his skin always feel so good against mine?

He added, "I'm the problem. I'm aware. I hoped mating with a siren would help me escape from my past, but I've been in the dark for so long that your light fucking hurts."

My chest tightened, and I opened my eyes. "I'm not trying to hurt you."

"I know." His lips brushed my bare shoulder, where he'd bitten me, and I shuddered. "No more nudity in front of my pack. You're mine."

"Just because you repeat that doesn't make it true. It doesn't mean I have to play along, either."

His teeth scraped my shoulder, and his erection slid between my thighs when I arched my back. One of his hands lifted to my throat, cupping the black band around my neck lightly. "This mark makes it true. The bite, too. And do I need to remind you about the way I claimed you in front of my pack, Isabella? You *are* mine."

"I go by Izzy. If you want to bring that up, you're technically mine too. And if you're mine, I get to feed from you whenever I want. You can't claim me without being claimed *by* me too."

He nipped at my shoulder again lightly. "You haven't bitten me."

"I'm a siren. I don't bite."

"The way you dug your nails into that chair tells me that I'll wear your mark another way."

My face flushed. "Screw off, bastard."

"The only thing I want to screw is you." He stepped forward, and I bit back a groan when the motion pushed his erection deeper against my ass.

"You're insane."

"I never claimed not to be."

He stepped us forward again, and again.

My breasts met the tile wall, and I sucked in a breath. "You like taking me from behind, don't you?"

"I *am* a wolf."

"I'm not. If we screw, I'm going to feed on you. While you knot me, so you can't pull away."

He growled. "Isabella..."

"It's Izzy."

He pulled my abdomen away from the wall just long enough to slip his hand between my thighs, and I bit my lip *hard* as he dragged a finger over my clit. "I don't have to knot you."

"You could finish on my ass," I agreed. "But I don't think you have the restraint to pull out. How many times did you get off when you knotted me? Six? Seven?"

"So fucking many." He teased my clit slowly, and my entire body seemed to clench.

Shit, I wanted him.

"Is that a yes?" he asked.

"No. You still abandoned me right after we had sex, and I know for a fact that wolves like to snuggle just as much as sirens."

"I shouldn't have done that. It was a mistake." He dragged his finger over my clit, and I fought hard not to let myself buck my hips.

"Mistake or not, you don't get to screw me without agreeing to let me feed from you whenever I want. Give me permission, and an apology for last night on top of it, or get out of my shower," I gritted out.

Porter pressed harder against my clit.

He knew exactly how to make me crazy, and he'd learned way too fast.

"You want an apology?"

"Yes. You're not taking me again without an apology."

"Even if I don't apologize, you'll eventually give in. I remember you telling me there would be sex, or you would be finding someone else to sate yourself with."

I leaned away from the wall long enough to pull his hand out from between my thighs and push it away. He set it back on my hip, but his grip was tighter.

"I'm stubborn enough that I won't give in. And considering your utter lack of self-control, I've now learned that I can't find someone else to sate me. My vibrator will have to do," I shot back. "I'm not kidding, Porter. I'm not someone you can use or a fuck buddy you can ditch after screwing when you want to take a stroll in the forest. I'm your mate. If you want to have sex with me, you have to respect me."

"Of course I respect you." There was a growl in his voice.

"How can you possibly think I believe that? You've been trying to push me around and use me since the day we met."

"That's not true."

"It is. And until you're ready to admit it and apologize, there will *not* be more sex." I turned around in his arms, and gestured toward the shower's entrance. "Now, get out."

I wasn't sure I'd gone from being the one who insisted there would be sex to the one refusing to give it to him, but there I was.

He slowly released my hips. His jaw was clenched, and his eyes were darker than ever. But when I gestured again, he finally turned and strode out of the shower. I couldn't help but shiver when I watched the water trail down his back and over his ass.

He had to be the most gorgeous man in the world. It was a shame his personality was so insanely difficult.

He stopped before leaving the bathroom, and turned to face me. "If I catch you getting yourself off, whether in person or through our mental bond, I *will* fuck you. The only thing that gets to fill you is me."

"That's insane," I shot back.

"I don't care. You're mine."

He finally left the room.

The door slammed behind him, and I let out a furious huff.

I turned back to the wall, pressing my forehead to it and ignoring the throbbing between my thighs.

I was going to get him back for that.

Oh, the bastard was going to *regret* teasing me.

IZZY

AFTER I SHOWERED, I had to go to the cafeteria to grab some food. Once again, I was met by a crowd of my new fans. And more slightly uncomfortable, sexual presents.

As bizarre as the situation was, I couldn't say I truly minded the gifts. Who didn't like opening presents?

Evan and Kim found me after about thirty minutes of inching away from my loving fans. Though I usually had no problem tapping into my bitchy side to get myself space, the wolves had been through hell. Curtis had hurt them—physically, a lot of the time. Mentally and emotionally, too.

I couldn't be one more person who treated them poorly. I refused.

So, I accepted presents. And chatted. And thanked them when they complimented me. And told them I was glad to help when they thanked me.

But I was really, really glad when the couple intervened, because there were a lot more people there for dinner than had been there for breakfast. I would've been there all night.

Evan told everyone he needed me for some alpha business, and Kim towed me out of the room while Evan went back for my food. I told him what I wanted through the pack bond, and thanked him when he met us in the hallway with it.

They led me to the alpha's office, which was only one door down from my new bedroom, and closed the door behind us.

I collapsed in the largest desk chair, digging into my food immediately.

"Where's Porter?" Evan asked.

I let out a frustrated breath. "We got in another fight. I don't know what to do with him. I don't want to hurt him any more than he's already hurting—but I can't let my mate treat me like shit. I won't. This whole situation is just a mess. I should've known better."

"What are you fighting about?" Evan asked.

I took a frustrated bite of my food. "He won't share a bed with me. Or apologize for ditching me after we screwed last night. He thinks he didn't do anything wrong."

"What was his reasoning?" Evan checked.

Kim didn't seem entirely interested in the conversation, so I felt a little bad about dragging her in, but Evan was asking questions.

"He said he needed time to think." I took another bite, and said with a full mouth, "I'm fucking done. How do I get off this train?"

"You don't," Kim said, entirely unempathetic. "You're the one who decided to board it."

"That was clearly a mistake."

"Mistakes have consequences. This one is yours." Kim leaned back in her seat.

She wasn't wrong.

"It wasn't a mistake," Evan said, frowning at his fiancée. "Coming back from hell takes time, but we'll get him back. Let me think of another way to make him jealous."

"No. Not this time. If he wants to be a dick, you have to let him. Making him jealous won't help. I'm not ready to deal with him like that right now."

Evan sighed. "Alright, I'll give it a few days. But if he doesn't come back, we enact the plan."

"That's fine," I agreed, then leaned toward him. "Has he really ordered his wolves not to let me leave Wolf Manor?"

Evan grimaced.

"Great." I took another bite.

Evan's eyes glazed over for a moment before he perked up. "Porter said he just got off the phone with the vampires. A group of them are coming with your sisters in a few days, to purify the lake with you."

I raised my eyebrows. "He didn't go back to the forest?"

"Apparently not." His voice was upbeat.

I didn't feel quite as cheerful as he seemed, so I just focused on my food. I finished quickly, and stood up. "I think I'm going to call it a night. Thanks for the rescue."

"Any time," Evan promised.

Kim murmured her agreement, and I slipped out of the office, padding down the hall.

As soon as I opened the door to my room and took a step inside, I froze.

Porter was sitting on the bed, his back to the pillows and his arms folded. His long, strong legs were sprawled out in front of him, and there was a dark look in his eyes.

They were on mine immediately.

I let out a slow breath, finally stepping inside and closing the door. "I didn't think I'd see you for a few days."

"I didn't either."

"Then what are you doing here?"

"You said you were hungry." He clenched his jaw for a moment, then slowly released it. "And I owe you an apology."

My eyebrows lifted. "I'm listening."

"You're right. I haven't treated you properly. I've been a shitty mate. You deserve better, but you have me, and there's no going back." Porter moved to the edge of the bed, setting his feet on the floor and standing up. "I shouldn't have left you the way I did. I was afraid of what was going to happen, and uncertain how I should act, but I shouldn't have left. I'm sorry."

"Thank you for apologizing." I slipped my hands into my pockets.

His forehead creased, and I knew he was waiting for me to tell him that it was okay or something.

"I don't forgive people immediately," I said. "If you want me to forgive you, you have to prove that you mean it by changing your behavior. I can't trust you right now. But I do appreciate your apology."

His eyes darkened, but he stiffly dipped his head. "You want me to stay here while you fall asleep?"

"I want you to communicate where you are and what you're doing if you're not going to be in our room with me at night. Mated men aren't supposed to be comfortable leaving their mates when they're asleep. It makes me feel like you're cheating on me." The admission made me feel a little vulnerable, and I wrapped my arms around my middle.

"I would never—could never—want another woman. I haven't been with anyone but you since I lost my family. I just have to run at night. It's how I'm coping with being back. If I stay here, I won't be able to sleep at all. Out there, I run until I collapse, and manage an hour or two of rest."

I didn't like the admission. It didn't make me feel any better about spending my nights alone. But I couldn't force him to do something else. "Do you run with anyone?"

"No. No one can keep up with me."

At least he wasn't secretly bonding with some bombshell shifter woman when he was away from me.

Probably.

I didn't have a real argument anymore, so I agreed with him. "Fine. I need to install a canopy on my bed."

His forehead creased. "A canopy?"

I nodded. "You know, like a coffin lid? I'm basically an emotional vampire."

Understanding crossed his face. "You didn't get much sleep last night?"

"No."

"I'll talk to Hale and get one sent over as soon as possible."

"Thanks."

He waved me closer. "You need to feed."

Right.

He wasn't going to be able to let me drink from him for long when he was already frustrated, but I couldn't point that out.

Part of me wanted to tell him I wasn't hungry, but he would've realized I was being a chicken.

So, I just kissed him.

I didn't bother parting his lips with my tongue, and he didn't either.

I managed a few pulls of his emotions before he pulled away from me with his jaw clenched, and left the room.

There had been no conversations about sex—and I almost wished there were. At least then, he'd show emotion.

THE CANOPY WAS DELIVERED HALF an hour later, while I was still lying in bed. The wolves who brought it to me left it at the door, saying they couldn't enter the alpha's rooms, which left me to figure out how to set it up on my own.

Zora and I were the ones who usually put things together, but the canopy's wiring was far beyond my level of knowledge. I ended up just wrestling with it myself until I managed to slip under it on my own.

With the comforting darkness surrounding me, I fell asleep fast. Thankfully, I slept through the night.

THE NEXT MORNING, I heard the door open while I was still in bed with the canopy down. I had spent the last two hours buried in the pack link, even though my head ached with hunger.

I still needed to figure out who the people were who wanted me dead.

And how much danger I was in.

They seemed to have figured out how to keep their plans quieter, though, because I barely felt their whispers. I couldn't find the consciousnesses behind the plots like I had before, and couldn't track them back to the source.

It was endlessly frustrating, and made me feel like I was starving.

"That doesn't look right," Porter said, his voice low and gravelly. I heard him open what sounded like the cover over the wiring part I hadn't even come close to figuring out.

I debated letting him know I was awake and getting out of bed, but didn't want to fight with him again. So I stayed quiet, lingering in the pack's bond.

My attention was split between the alpha and the pack as Porter quietly figured out the wiring and got it working properly. It had probably been an hour when he finally used the button outside to lift the canopy.

I opened my eyes slowly, feigning sleep, and couldn't help but notice the way his gaze softened as it moved over me.

"Good morning," he said.

"Morning," I murmured.

Part of me waited for him to bring up what he'd done for me and use it against me or something.

Instead, he said, "I didn't feed you long enough last night."

I blinked.

Right.

That's what he was there for.

I'd be glad to get free of my headache, but part of me was disappointed that he hadn't just shown up because he wanted to see me or something.

That part of me was ridiculous, so I stuffed it down.

"Yeah," I finally said.

He sat down on the edge of the bed and offered me his hand. "We shouldn't have to kiss for you to feed now that we're mated."

"Right."

I put my hand on his arm and tried to use my magic the way I usually did when I kissed people. It sprang to life immediately, and my eyes shut automatically as his intense, dark emotions hit me again.

The man was a drug, and I was his willing addict.

He pulled away when he couldn't handle it anymore, and left the room before I could thank him.

I collapsed on the pillow, panting as I stared up at the ceiling.

What would it feel like to live in a mind that dark?

Would I be any kinder, more involved, or more enthusiastic than he was if I did?

My anger toward him faded a little as I considered it... because no. I wouldn't be.

If I was barely clinging to my sanity the way he was, I would be just as bad as him.

And that meant I needed to start showing him a little more compassion, even though I still had to hold to my boundaries.

THE NEXT WEEK PASSED QUICKLY.

I only saw Porter in passing, other than the next time he fed me as briefly as possible. He spoke to me through the mate bond to let me know where he was and what he was doing from time to time. I told him I was swimming, and sent him mental images of myself in my swimsuit.

I hoped the images would push him to act again, but no dice.

Eight days had gone by when my sisters finally managed a visit. The lake was already a little less murky than it had been when I arrived, but after I spent all day swimming with my sisters, it would get much better.

I waited for them in the hallway where Wolf Manor met the neutral territory, leaning up against the wall. Porter joined me around the time I got Clementine's text that they were on their way, and I couldn't stop myself from tapping my foot as the minutes passed.

"You're excited," Porter said, watching me closely.

"Of course I'm excited. This is the longest I've been away from all of my sisters in more than a decade. They're all I have at this point."

"You have me."

"Do I?" I lifted an eyebrow.

His expression changed, but the security doors opened before I could decide what he might've felt in response to the question.

My attention snapped back to them in time to see two large vampire guards come through. Clementine stepped around them, her whole face lighting up when she saw me.

I couldn't help but grin as I caught her, hugging her fiercely.

"Vamp Manor isn't the same without you," she said into my hair. "Can we break you out of here?"

I laughed, though I heard Porter's mostly suppressed growl. "No, but I miss you too."

I wouldn't offer to let my sisters move to the wolves' land unless they asked. And in that case, I'd have to talk to Porter to make sure there was a way to keep them safe. But honestly, Vamp Manor seemed like the safest place for them, and I wanted them safe more than I wanted to keep them with me.

Plus, Blair would be alone if they left.

Granted, she did have friends in Vamp Manor. And Hale. She was ridiculously in love with him, and he was even crazier about her.

So maybe she'd be fine just seeing our sisters when we all met up.

But Wolf Manor still wasn't safe for an unmated siren. Which meant it didn't particularly matter where they wanted to be. The vampires were the only real option.

"Did she turn down the break-out?" Zora asked Clem, as she threw her arms around me next.

"She did," I confirmed.

Zora gave a dramatic sigh. "Bitch."

"I know. You love me anyway."

"You know I do."

Avery stepped into my arms after Zora moved, hugging me just as tightly as the others had. "The roof misses you," she murmured.

"You should *not* be up there alone."

"Blair's turning it into a mini-golf course, so the construction stuff keeps me hidden."

"It does not."

She pulled away, a little mischief on her face as she lifted her finger to her lips in the universal sign for "*shh*".

"We'll keep her off the roof," Zora said, eyeing Avery suspiciously.

"She's fine. We have cameras there," Blair countered,

replacing Avery as she hugged me last. "I expect more phone calls soon."

"I didn't get a phone call," Clementine protested.

"You're not mated. You don't know the secrets," Blair teased.

Clem feigned offence, lifting her hand to her chest. "I'd better find myself a mate."

"You'd better not. I will *not* survive the vampires without you," Zora warned.

"Let's get moving," Avery suggested. "We can have this talk while we clean out Izzy's lake."

"Is there a bunch of junk in it?" Clementine asked.

"No. I've pulled out a few random things. A shoe here, a pair of underwear there. A few glass bottles, too. But it's so murky, it's really hard to say for sure."

"Would you be able to keep your wolves away from the lake if we tapped into our magic more than usual?" Blair asked, and it took me a minute to realize she was talking to Porter. "It would pull anyone nearby to us, but we could clean the lake much faster."

I looked sideways at him, waiting for him to stonewall her, but he just nodded. "That wouldn't be a problem."

His easy agreement surprised me.

"Awesome," Blair said.

A glance in their direction showed that her and Hale were holding hands again.

I was happy for her, even if my own mate was more like an acquaintance who had screwed me really, really well on one occasion.

"How many hours do you think it'll take if you turn your magic up?" Hale asked.

Blair shrugged and looked at me.

Everyone else did too. I could feel their eyes, even though we were still moving.

"All day, probably," I admitted. "It's pretty bad."

"We should've brought chlorine, to make it a real party," Clem said.

Hale and Zora snorted.

Blair and Avery grinned.

I made a face.

"Why would chlorine affect anything?" Porter asked, still looking at me.

When no one else rushed to explain it to him, I shrugged. "It reacts strangely with our magic. When we swim in chlorinated water, we end up covered *everywhere* in glitter that can't be scrubbed off. It takes like two weeks for all of it to fall off. It's a pain in the ass."

Suddenly, there was interest in his eyes.

Too much interest.

The look reminded me of Hale saying that Porter used to be wild and rebellious, which made me narrow my eyes at him.

He went back to being neutral a moment later, but I'd noticed the change.

And while I was suddenly a little suspicious, part of me was proud. Because finally, I'd seen another glimpse of the real Porter.

WE HAD to walk to the lake like humans, because tapping into our speed could still set off the chase instinct in any wolf who saw us moving fast. It was kind of a long walk, but it was so good to talk to my sisters again that I enjoyed every minute of it.

When we reached the water, my sisters were all just as excited as I'd been the first day. Porter cleared out the area nearby, and we dove in, turning our magic up as high as we could.

We'd all need to feed when we finally left the water—but it would be worth it.

ten

PORTER

I FORCED myself to breathe through the intensity of my mate's magic. My fists were clenched, my cock throbbing painfully, and I couldn't stop myself from imagining having my mate's body around mine in every way there was.

"You good?" Hale asked, watching me closely. We sat on beach chairs just outside the lake, with the sun shining down on us.

"Can't you feel Blair's magic?" I gritted out.

"Yeah. Feels fucking good." He flashed me a grin. "But she knew this was a possibility and prepared me for it."

He'd undoubtedly sated himself on her blood and screwed her. Repeatedly.

The way I wanted to with Izzy.

Hell, the way I *needed* to.

I was on the verge of mentally calling her back to the surface and taking her into the trees so I could have my way with her. Being able to think straight again for a few minutes afterward sounded like a necessity.

But I knew her well enough to be sure that asking would result with an immediate *no*.

Which would hurt.

"So you're not good?" Hale checked.

"I'm fine."

"The moon's almost full. I can't imagine that's making staying in control any easier."

I grunted in response.

It didn't. The full moon was the next night, and I had no doubt it was going to cause me even more problems with my mate.

He added, "You sound like you're in pain. We can move further from the water. It'll help."

I wanted to ease the pressure, but I couldn't go further from my mate. I needed to stay close to her, to protect her.

Not to mention, her magic was urging me to dive into the water and not come up until I'd found her. Which would obviously kill me, because I couldn't see a damn thing down there.

"You should be at least a little used to her magic at this

point." He studied me a little more closely. "You *have* felt it before, haven't you?"

"No. I feed her before she gets hungry," I gritted out. "And she's good at keeping it under control."

"Even if she is, it shouldn't be affecting you this badly if you're screwing. You are, aren't you?"

I stared at the lake. He didn't need an answer.

It wasn't this business what I was or wasn't doing with my mate.

"Damn, man. No wonder it's hitting you so hard." He grinned. "You're not going to last all day. Wave her over the next time they surface, and tell her the truth."

"If that worked on your mate this soon after you met her, she's a different kind of woman than mine."

Hale chuckled. "Fair point."

"How long did it take you?"

"To win her over? Longer than I would've liked. She only hated me for a few weeks, but from there, it was a while before she was willing to even consider having feelings for me. When they were young teenagers, Blair's father killed all of their mothers out of some deluded idea of love. They joke about taking mates sometimes, but I don't think any of them have ever had a reason to really *believe* in mate bonds."

"Even your mate?"

His smile widened. "Well, she does now."

Fuck, the thought made my chest ache.

Knowing that my mate didn't have that, and it was my fault, fucking hurt. I needed to do better.

Two of the women's heads popped up in the middle of the lake. I recognized my mate immediately, noticing that her light hair was braided back the same way it had been the day Arthur touched her. One of her sisters must've done it under the water.

The one with her had curly hair. I was pretty sure it was Zora, but none of them had bothered introducing themselves to me.

Straining my ears, I tried to hear the conversation but only caught a few words.

Weak.

Hungry.

One of them clearly needed to feed.

The way they both looked at me told me which of them it was.

Isabella shook her head and disappeared back beneath the water.

I let out a harsh breath, unable to stop myself from reaching my mind out to hers.

"If you're feeling weak, come up here and let me feed you." The words came out sharper than I intended.

"I'm fine."

I could feel that she was lying.

Force didn't achieve anything with her, so I didn't bother going that route. Instead, I asked,

"Won't the lake be purified much faster if you have more power to use on it?"

She huffed. *"You're trying to goad me into feeding on you, and it's not going to work."*

"Alright."

I withdrew, though I was fairly confident I'd just won the battle.

She *really* wanted the lake purified.

TEN HELLISH MINUTES LATER, her head finally broke the surface of the water right by us.

The intensity of her magic had me closing my eyes and breathing through the fierce need that pounded through me. My cock fucking hurt. My balls, too.

"What's wrong with him?" she asked Hale.

"He's horny."

"It can't be that bad."

"I don't think he's ever felt your magic before, so yeah, it can. Incoming full moon doesn't help."

A pair of small, soft hands combed my hair away from my face, and I couldn't suppress my groan. The pressure of her magic eased a little, but her presence erased any relief I may have had.

When I opened my eyes and found myself face-to-face with her breasts, straining against her black bikini while the water on them caught the light, I gripped the chair's armrests tighter.

"I'm getting a phone call," Hale said, and the words barely registered.

Some part of me heard him walking away, but I couldn't tear my gaze from my mate.

She sat down on my lap, and her eyes replaced her breasts in my immediate line of sight. The pressure of her body against my cock made everything hurt more—and feel better too, at the same time.

Surprisingly enough, she looked amused.

"I didn't think my magic would affect you."

"Then why have you kept it under wraps since we bonded?" I gritted out.

Her amusement faded. "Habit."

One of her hands was still in my hair, and she tried to use it to pull my face to hers.

I resisted. "If you kiss me, I'm going to lose complete control of myself."

Her eyes gleamed. "Sounds like fun."

One of my chair's armrests snapped beneath my hand, and her lips curved upward.

When she pulled my face to hers again, I didn't resist.

I didn't want to.

I *couldn't.*

eleven

IZZY

PORTER TASTED LIKE SALT.

He'd been sweating as he fought my magic.

I didn't know why that turned me on so much, but it did.

And unlike the last time I kissed him, this time, he took charge.

His tongue was rough against mine, his kiss brutal and demanding. His hands found my ass immediately, and he pulled me down harder, grinding me against his erection.

I hadn't even touched his emotions yet, and he'd already lost hold of his iron willpower.

And to be honest, it made me feel powerful.

I finally drank from him, and the feeling was like an electric shock.

I arched against him, and his hands slid beneath my bikini bottoms, gripping my bare ass.

He pulled me against him harder, and I could feel every inch of his erection.

Damn, I wanted him.

He snarled into my mouth as I pulled harder on his emotions, and a heartbeat later, he filled me with three of his fingers.

I gasped, releasing his emotions for a moment, but he didn't stop kissing me.

He pulled his fingers out a little before driving them back in, and I arched against them hard. His cock was still against my clit, and felt amazing.

But I wanted more.

Flexing my power again, I lifted my hips enough to free his cock. He got the message immediately, sliding his fingers out of me. I felt the backs of his claws as he shifted them just long enough to slice through my swim bottoms—then pulled me down over his erection.

I sucked in a breath at the sudden pressure, and held it as my body adjusted to his size.

Wow.

Yeah.

It had been way too long since he'd been inside me.

Way. Too. Long.

I finally breathed out, and took another long pull of his emotions.

He snarled, slamming me down harder.

Driving himself in deeper.

He bottomed out inside me, and my hands found his shoulders. My fingers dug into his shirt.

He lifted me and pulled me back down again, and again, until I was finally crying out in pleasure as my body tightened around him.

Porter snarled as he came with me, the base of his cock swelling and thickening. My sounds of pleasure became screams of bliss as my orgasm went on and on.

I was fully sated when I came down from the high, and entirely overwhelmed with feeling him inside me as deep as he was. His knot was hard against my g-spot, and making my world spin a little from the intensity.

"Shit," I breathed.

"You're fighting it again." His voice was low and animalistic.

"I don't know how to stop."

"Can I end my phone call yet?" Hale called, far enough away that his voice was faint.

"No!" I yelled, at the same time Porter snarled the word.

"Got it," Hale hollered.

My chest rose and fell rapidly as Porter pulled my hands off him long enough to tug his t-shirt over his head and yank it down over mine.

"Feels like we've been in this situation before," I panted, setting my hands back down on Porter's bare shoulders.

"I was wearing less clothing last time." His hands slid up my abdomen, finding my breasts and moving over my bikini top. "So were you."

"It's still good, though."

"Perfect." His hand slid between us, and I groaned when he teased my clit. "Let go, Isabella. Drink from me if it helps."

"You hate that."

"I love it. I just have a hard time handling it in large amounts." He pressed hard against my clit, making my hips jerk. "You deserve the pleasure I can give you if you let go."

"Do I?"

"Hell yes. I'm going to be inside you for the next twenty minutes—just think about how many times I can make you come."

"You *are* good at that."

"Just look into my eyes and focus on the way your body feels, baby."

"I'm not your baby," I breathed, as I neared my edge again.

"Whatever you say." He dragged his thumb around my clit,

and I jerked my hips, swearing at the slight burn as his knot wedged deeper. "Drink from me."

The command caught me by surprise enough that I followed it, tugging on his emotions. And the moment I tasted him, I lost it, taking him over the edge with me as I did.

After that second climax, I was putty in his hands.

He brought me to climax again and again, until his knot finally softened and the magic holding us faded.

"Shit," I gasped, lifting my hands away from his shoulders and finding blood beneath my nails. "Holy shit. I'm sorry."

"Don't apologize. That was incredible." His hands slid down my waist and over the curve of my bare ass. "I'll send someone to get you a new pair of swim bottoms."

I wrinkled my nose. "No way. I don't want someone going through my swimsuits. And you don't like having people in our room. You can just give me your shirt when I get out of the lake."

His eyes narrowed. "Not happening. Definitely not while your magic is doing what it's doing."

"What do you suggest, then?"

"I carry you to our room, and you change there."

"Absolutely not. I am *full* of your release, remember?"

His lips curved upward, just a little.

It was one of the first smiles I'd seen from him, if not the very first, and it lit up his entire gorgeous face.

"I remember."

"Then give me a better option, or we're going with mine."

His hands moved over my ass slowly, making me want to curl into him even more than I already was. "I'll run back for the swimsuit. You stay in the water. When I get back, you put it on underwater. The pack's already away, and Hale will come back over so he's nearby just in case."

"Finally, a reasonable solution." I patted his ridiculously thick pectorals. "Deal.

A squeal escaped me when he stood up suddenly. I clutched his body as he carried me to the edge of the water, lifted me off his erection, and unceremoniously dropped me in.

The lake was already significantly clearer than it had been before, but deep enough that it still hid my nudity as I sat on the rough sand with water up to my chin.

"I'll be back soon. Stay right there." His words were neutral, but there was a bit of warning in his voice that I didn't think I'd ever heard before. Something about the show of emotions made me want to push him harder, but I rolled my eyes and nodded.

He shifted, ditching his clothes before he took off toward the manor.

I watched him leave—and Hale stride back to retake his chair. The rest of the guards were far enough away from the lake that we couldn't see them, but close enough that I was pretty sure they were patrolling the forest around it to make sure my sisters stayed safe.

"Can't say I expected that," Hale remarked.

"You and me both." I looked back out at the water, letting out a slow breath as my body tingled with the memory of the way Porter had felt.

"You ready for the full moon?"

"No. No one tells me a damn thing here unless I ask, and it hasn't occurred to me. When is it?"

"Tomorrow."

"Great." I lifted a hand to my hair, dragging my hand over the smooth braids Clementine had done for me. "Any clues?"

"Not really. All I know is that the wolves are reduced to their most feral form. A little like fae during their eclipses."

"Let's cross our fingers they all just go furry and spend the whole night running around in the forest, then," I said.

He chuckled. "It would be better to ask your mate."

"He avoids me, so I don't know when I'd get a chance to do that. The bastard won't even share a bed with me."

Hale whistled. "Stubborn asshole."

"I know."

"Have you tried pushing him?"

"No. Evan wants me to, but I don't want to hurt him any more than he's already hurting."

"Sometimes you have to throw water over someone's face to wake them up. It's a similar principle."

"Jealousy doesn't seem like the right kind of water."

Hale snorted. "Who says you need jealousy? Igniting his possessiveness would do just as well, without risking anyone's life."

"Aren't they the same?"

"Not even close."

"What do you suggest, then?"

Hale's eyes gleamed wickedly. "There's a simple way to set off a mated male."

"I'm listening."

Hale explained a simple, but effective plan that made my stomach clench with what felt a hell of a lot like anticipation. He was done quickly, and smoothly changed the subject to the minigolf course Blair was building on the roof when I caught my first glimpse of Porter on his way back.

When Porter tossed me the only one-piece swimsuit I owned—the one that covered more skin than any other bathing suit I possessed—I rolled my eyes at him but swam out to pull it on. He caught the bikini top I threw back to him, and tucked it in his pocket before I slid beneath the waves to rejoin my sisters.

After my conversation with Blair's mate, I was actually looking forward to that night.

THE SUN WAS GOING down when we were all too drained to stay in the water any longer. It was damn near crystal clear, and I knew I could finish purifying it myself over the next week or two.

A few wolves brought dinner out for all of us, the same way they'd brought lunch, so we all feasted together before heading back to the Manor.

After a round of hugs and promises to call everyone, not just Blair, they left me in the hallway with Porter.

I missed them immediately—but had something else to look forward to.

"Do I need to be worried about the full moon tomorrow?" I asked Porter, as we walked to our room.

"No." His answer was immediate, and I shot him a look that said I needed more information. He clarified. "It'll be fine. I had someone install a thick, solid lock on our door. That will keep me and anyone else out all night, so it'll be normal for you."

"As opposed to..."

"Wild." He said the word without hesitation.

"How wild?" I pushed. "Orgies? Murder? Cannibalism? Human sacrifice?"

His lips twitched as he fought a grin. "None of the above. Except maybe the orgies—but those are rare. They usually happen so far on the outskirts of the forest that no one stumbles upon them."

"If you stumble upon one, I'll have to cut your dick off."

"You don't need to worry about that. The only person I want is you."

"Somehow, that's not convincing."

"You can access my mind freely throughout the night if you need to. I'll probably spend most of it trying to break into our room, so I doubt you'll find that necessary."

"Trying to *break into* our room?" We reached the door, but I stopped there without stepping inside. He was going to leave if I walked in.

"You're my mate." He lifted a shoulder. "In my basest form, I want you. Endlessly."

The words made my heart beat a little harder. Though I had a plan to push him (hopefully right into my bed) I hadn't actually asked him to sleep next to me.

Suddenly, that seemed like a pretty important step.

"Do you want to share the bed tonight?" I asked him, gesturing toward the door that I still hadn't opened. I didn't want to spook him when he'd already made it clear that he didn't want to share the room on multiple occasions.

"I do," he said, nodding once. Slowly. My hope inflated, just a little bit. "But I shouldn't."

The deflation was hard and fast.

I'd let myself get my hopes up far too soon.

"Alright. Goodnight." I stepped through the door, and he mirrored my goodbye as I shut it.

My eyes lingered on the new, extensive locking system, but I only turned the deadbolt. He had the code, so he could get through that if he changed his mind.

He didn't change his mind, though.

So, determination settled on my shoulders.

I pulled the one gifted vibrator I'd actually kept from my nightstand drawer, and slipped beneath the blankets.

Porter was going to change his mind about living with me the way mates were supposed to, or he was going to be tortured by the scent of my pleasure every time he stepped into our room.

It was his choice to make.

twelve

PORTER

THE NEXT MORNING, the pack was bustling with energy in preparation for the full moon that night. I brushed my mind against Isabella's long enough to learn that she was already in the cafeteria, having breakfast without me.

Though that irked me, I knew it only did so because of the incoming full moon.

And the mate bond.

Which was permanent.

I needed to do something about it if I didn't want to feel that every morning. But the only option I could think of would require spending my nights with my mate.

I wouldn't be able to maintain a hold on my sanity if I didn't spend those hours working myself hard in the forest, so that wasn't a real possibility.

Hence the way I'd turned her down the night before, when I wanted badly to take her up on the offer.

Though instinct told me to head straight to the cafeteria to join my mate, I reeked of sweat. I'd need to shower before I found her.

So, I went to our room.

I preferred it when my mate waited for me there, but I supposed she never really *waited* for me. I just usually got back early enough to catch her before she left.

Why couldn't I do that every day?

There really wasn't a reason.

I'd made up my mind to do exactly that, when I stepped into our room and halted just inside the doorway.

My nostrils flared immediately.

My nails shifted to claws, cutting into my palms as my fists clenched.

I had never fucked her in our room—but I could smell her release.

The door slammed shut behind me as I stormed across the room, flinging the comforter to the side and inhaling deeply.

If I smelled another man on our sheets, there would be carnage.

But all I smelled was her.

Some part of me was satisfied by that, though I didn't stop my search. I found the toy that smelled of her perfect little cunt in the drawer, and resisted the urge to destroy it.

It would be much better used to show her exactly who she belonged to. And who had the right to her climaxes.

It wasn't the fucking toy.

Dropping it back in the drawer, I strode out of the room without a glance backward, or at the shower.

Sweat was the last thing on my mind.

The only thing that mattered was my female. And she would *never* fuck herself without me again.

thirteen

IZZY

MY FOOT TAPPED IMPATIENTLY beneath the table.

I had another stack of sexual presents on my left, the same way I did every morning. I'd gotten the contact number for a women's shelter in Mistwood and had started sending the vibrators and dildos out there. I didn't know if they genuinely wanted them, but I definitely didn't need all of them.

And while I wasn't sure I'd ever be *tired* of getting presents, I was starting to hope the pack would move on from the gifts and just find a way to live life normally again.

Except Nora.

I ate the peppermint chocolate she gave me almost as fast as she handed it over, and it made her ridiculously happy every time I reached out to her for more through the pack link. I'd tried to pay her, but she refused to take my money.

The cafeteria's doors slammed open, and every eye in the room landed on the furious alpha in the doorway.

His eyes were wild, his hair was stuck to his forehead with sweat, and his chest was heaving roughly.

There was no question who he was there for.

And *yes*, I'd pissed him off just as much as I hoped.

All of the noise in the room died down as he stormed around the tables until he reached me. Then, without a word, he threw me over his shoulder and all but flew down the hall, toward our bedroom.

I didn't bother worrying about the presents. Someone would inevitably bring them to my room and leave them by the door.

"What's your problem?" I demanded, though there was no heat behind the words.

"You know exactly what my problem is, female," he growled, his hand tightening around my upper thigh in a way that made me hot.

"Do I?"

He slammed the door to our bedroom shut behind us, and tossed me onto the bed. I landed so lightly that I knew he'd been careful not to hurt me, despite his clear anger. "I told you not to get yourself off, and you filled yourself with this." He pulled the gigantic vibrator out of the drawer, his eyes still dark with fury.

"You weren't willing to take care of my needs yourself," I said bluntly. "What else was I supposed to do?"

"Tell me you needed me," he gritted out.

"I didn't need you. I had that." I gestured toward the toy.

He snarled, grabbing my knees and pulling me to the edge of the bed, so my legs hung off as he towered over me. Propping myself up on my arms, I waited for his next move. "You think this can make you feel as good as I can?"

No.

I knew it couldn't.

But it did the job anyway.

"Yes," I lied.

His eyes flashed like I'd challenged him.

He peeled my jeans down my legs, tore my panties off, and opened me wide. "You think this can make you scream the way I do, Isabella?"

"Yes," I breathed, as he put the tip of it against my entrance.

"Prove it." He slid it inside me, still gentle enough despite that fury, and my head tipped back as my hips arched with the sudden entrance.

He bottomed it out inside me, making me suck in a breath. My fingers dug into the blankets as he pulled it out and drove it back in a little rougher.

My hips arched.

My body rocked and moved.

He worked it in and out over and over, nudging my clit with the top part and finding my g-spot now and then.

But the feeling was nothing like having his cock inside me.

"You need more," he said.

"No," I panted, though he was right.

"You *deserve* more."

Yes, I did.

I deserved my mate in my bed, where he belonged.

I deserved not to have to worry if he was running with some furry bitch every night. Not to have to hope he hadn't gotten hurt somehow.

"If this was my cock, you would've already come twice." His voice was low and angry, but he was right, and we both knew it.

"Turn it on," I moaned, and he finally hit the button.

My hips arched, and I cried out as he pulled it away too soon.

Way too soon.

"You think I'm going to let you come on this toy again, Isabella?" He laughed humorlessly. "If you want your release, you take it wrapped around me."

"Fine. Fuck me."

"I haven't heard an apology yet."

"You're not getting one." My hips arched desperately, but he pulled the toy out before I could finish again, and I groaned.

"Then you aren't either."

I was talking about apologies—but he was talking about climaxes.

"Fuck you, Porter."

"You should've," he agreed, driving the toy in deep enough to make me gasp.

"You should've been in my bed, like a real mate. If you want to screw me, you sleep here with me."

His eyes locked with mine, and he held the vibrator where it was as my body tightened and my pleasure rose. Just before I could shatter, he pulled it out again, leaving my body desperate and aching.

He lifted the vibrator to his mouth and turned it off, then slowly licked my slickness off the length of it before he said, "I can't share your bed."

"Then you can't screw me again, or stop me from getting myself off."

He tucked the vibrator in his pocket and stepped back. "Touch yourself, and I tie your hands to the bed the next time we do this."

My chest rose and fell rapidly as his hot gaze moved over me slowly.

Carnally.

Needily.

"If you jerk off after this, I'm leaving," I said, the threat in my voice absolutely honest.

"I can't knot my hand, so I wouldn't be able to come if I tried."

"You can get off without knotting."

"Not anymore." With one last, long look at my soaked core, he strode out of the room. Over his shoulder, he called, "Don't open the door tonight, no matter what. If you go to the pool, be back here by noon. The moon madness sets in during the afternoon."

I lifted a hand to flip him off, even though I knew I'd do exactly what he said for the sake of my safety.

He left me on our bed, with my thighs open and my core drenched.

I was so furious, I could barely breathe.

If that bastard thought he could control me like that, he was in for a fucking show, because one thing was sure:

He had just declared war.

And a siren would never lose a lust war.

I SPENT the rest of the day and most of the night putting my plan together. Porter was right about him trying to break into my room while he was affected by the moon, so I distracted myself from the repetitive pounding and banging by texting my sisters.

Blair was probably sleeping or hooking up with Hale, so she didn't answer, but everyone else was there.

ME

Can one of you collect worn underwear that belongs to a few random vampire dudes who rarely leave Vamp Manor?

CLEM

On it

ZORA

WTF?

Not on it

Why?

ME

Porter declared war

Sex war

I can't invite random guys into my bed, because he'd kill them, but he won't be able to get to the vamps

CLEM

DEFINITELY on it

ZORA

Why did he declare a sex war?

AVERY

The better question is HOW did he declare a sex war?

> **ME**
>
> It's way tmi

CLEM

We're listening

I sighed, but typed out a quick summary.

> **ME**
>
> Hale told me if I got myself off, he would smell it afterward and it would piss him off enough that he'd end up sleeping in bed with me. I did. He lost his shit and used the vibrator to make me horny, didn't get me off, then threatened me and left

CLEM

Like a sexy threat?

> **ME**
>
> I guess

ZORA

I don't even like sex, but now I'm kind of thinking that this war sounds fun

> **ME**
>
> It would be more fun to actually have sex
>
> And have my mate sleep with me like he's supposed to

CLEM

We'll get you so many pairs of dirty underwear

AVERY

Zora just snorted so hard, water came out of her nose

ME

LOL

Thank you

You guys are the best

CLEM

kiss-blowing emoji

AVERY

We'll send one of the vamps over with
them in the morning

ZORA

Are there any other steps to winning
this war?

ME

Definitely

ZORA

I can imagine the evil grin on your face,
and I'm totally here for it

ME

But if the underwear works, I won't need
the other steps

CLEM

Not gonna lie, I hope it doesn't work

AVERY

Clementine…

ME

I hope it doesn't work too. I want to make
this bastard suffer.

ZORA

Damn, she means business

ME

He did tell me we could only be business
or pleasure, and he picked the former

And he's definitely going to regret it

CLEM

Keep us updated!

And tell us if Porter disposes of the
underwear so you need more

ME

I will

Love you

ZORA

Love you

CLEM

Love you!

AVERY

Love you. Don't do anything irreversible

ME

I won't

Probably

After a minute, I sent one more message.

ME

How much would you guys judge me if I
got a clitoral hood piercing for the sake of
this war?

Their answers made me laugh so hard, I heard Porter
howling through the door.

The bastard could be as loud as he wanted—I wasn't opening it for him.

MY PACKAGE ARRIVED with a knock the next morning. I pulled the door open carefully, peeking outside until I saw Porter asleep on the floor, completely naked in his human form, and snoring loudly.

I could've thrown a towel or blanket over him, but my feelings toward him weren't the loving or helpful kind at the moment. So, he didn't get a towel.

I quietly accepted the package from the drowsy wolf dude who'd stepped over Porter. He nodded at me before heading down the hallway, and my heart pounded like a drum as I slipped back inside with the goods.

The grin stretching across my face was so massive, it nearly hurt.

The plan was disgusting—but it would work, and no one would die. Probably.

So, it was worth it.

AFTER HIDING the unfortunate goods everywhere, I slipped out of the room and made my way to the pond. I didn't see any wolves up and moving yet, so I tapped into my enhanced speed to get me there as fast as possible.

Porter was going to be livid when he woke up, and I wasn't going to be in the room when he did.

Sex wars could be fought at a distance.

Partially, at least.

The next stage in my plan would require a little more hands-on effort, but I definitely wasn't dreading that. There was no way in hell that Porter was going to let me sleep in our bedroom alone when it smelled like both my pleasure and other men. Not a single chance. And I'd made sure to hide the underwear so thoroughly that *everything* would smell.

Our clothes.

Our shoes.

Our toilet paper.

Our towels.

Our sheets and blankets.

Our pillows.

The bedframe and box springs beneath our mattress.

Yeah, I was golden.

And Porter was going to lose his mind. Giddiness had me grinning at the thought.

I stripped out of my bikini and dropped it beneath a tree, diving into the gorgeous blue water. It was almost clear— and if I tapped into my magic, I could make it better.

There was no reason to let Porter believe we weren't at war after what he'd done, so I went ahead and pulled my magic to the surface. Not all of it—I didn't want anyone drowning themselves in their desperation to find me beneath the water—but enough.

Any wolf who came nearby would feel it.

They wouldn't be able to reach me, of course. But they'd want to.

If Porter thought *he* would have the upper hand in a sex war, he was deluded.

Fur had nothing on siren magic.

IZZY

I PAID close attention to the lake as I purified the water. If anyone put themselves in danger, I'd have to stop, of course. Clothing was the only acceptable casualty in a war of sex. Underwear in particular.

Thankfully, the wolves who were pulled in by my magic stayed close to the shore, just hanging out in the water without searching for me.

I heard Porter's snarl through our mental bond, and my lips stretched in a wicked smile.

Served the bastard right.

"What did you do?" he demanded.

"I told you I didn't want to sleep alone."

"I'll kill every fucking man whose scent is in our room."

"MY room, you mean? You've never slept there. And good luck."

He wasn't going to get into Vamp Manor while he was raging, even if he lost control of himself enough to try. Which I didn't really think would happen.

I was close enough to his mind to hear a hesitant female consciousness brush against Porter's mind, distracting him from his fury. *"Alpha? This probably isn't the best time to tell you, but you said you wanted to be alerted…"*

"What?" he asked sharply.

"Much of the pack is feeling your mate's magic luring us toward the lake."

He roared so loudly, it rang through the pack's link.

I grinned widely.

This war was mine.

"Thanks for letting me know," he forced out.

"Yeah."

Their connection ended, and I pulled back. Porter followed me to my mind immediately. *"What the fuck are you doing, Isabella?"*

"You declared a sex war. It's not my fault if you regret the outcome," I drawled.

"I sure as hell didn't declare a sex war. What does that even mean?"

"You threatened me not to get myself off after taking me to the edge, then walked away. What did you think it was going to accomplish? Pissing me off? I'm not the kind of woman you can

walk all over, asshole. I've been nice because of the hell you've been through, but I'm done. You started the war—I just made it official."

"End it," he demanded.

I laughed humorlessly. *"I'm having way too much fun for that, alpha."*

He snarled into my mind again, and I knew he was coming for me. *"I'll end it for you."*

Good fucking luck.

I made my way to the deepest part of the lake. In general, magical beings could hold their breath longer than humans, which meant there was a good chance he could reach me, even down there. It wasn't any deeper than the pool in Vamp Manor, and I knew the vampires could swim to the bottom of that. Which meant Porter could probably reach me.

But the lake was a lot wider than the pool.

And though the water was clear, there were no lights to help him see to the bottom, which meant I'd be hidden.

Our mate bond *did* mean he could somehow feel my location at all times, but I wasn't sure whether that would help him or not. Only time would tell. I'd never tapped into that particular part of our bond's magic myself, so I didn't know how it worked.

I heard Porter's command ring through the pack's link as I settled against the bottom of the lake. His magic had never felt so strong before. It cut through the half-assed hold of my magic's lure like butter.

"Everyone will get away from and stay away from the lake until tonight," he commanded, his voice ringing with authority. *"If you feel my mate's magic, shift and run into the forest until you're free of it."*

I felt the pack's agreement. Even those who didn't like him much or wanted me dead respected his power, and fell into line.

Just in case he could locate me, I swam around slowly. I wasn't giving him control over me while I was in the lake. Not even a little.

When I knew the people around me had been given enough time to get away, I strengthened the pull of my magic. Porter growled into my mind in response, and I smiled.

I paid close attention to the surface of the water above me, waiting for the inevitable feeling of the alpha diving in.

Sure enough, his smooth entry into the water caught my attention a few minutes later.

I waited until he had nearly reached me before shooting away in the opposite direction. The rapid motion would trigger his instinct to chase me, but considering our bond and the pull of my magic, that didn't really matter.

He surfaced, and when he disappeared from the water, I focused on the top long enough to realize he'd gotten in the boat I'd seen tied to the dock so many times.

It either belonged to him, or he'd commandeered it. Both seemed equally possible.

"Do you realize the situation we're in?" he growled into my mind. *"We can spend the entire day here while I try to fish you out and haul you back to our room. Or you can just come up here and talk to me."*

"When has that ever worked for me with you? Every time we talk, you end up basically telling me that what I feel and want doesn't matter compared to what you feel and want. Why should I give in to you yet again, and give you even more power over me?"

"I have no fucking power over you," he snarled back. *"When have you ever done what I wanted?"*

"You're holding me captive in your pack. Forcing me to sleep in your room, despite my lack of comfort here and my repeated requests for you to share it. Only feeding me when you want to. You bound my mind to yours and your pack without asking me or warning me." I paused for a moment, my body trembling slightly with my anger, before I went on.

"You've left me to deal with the pack's link—hearing half of them despise me and half obsess over me, daily—on my own. I've tried to be patient and understanding, but the only thing you've ever done for me is ask my sisters to come for the day. You don't even call me by the name I choose to go by. Everything is always about you. So don't fucking try to tell me that you don't have power over me. I agreed to be your mate, but I've been dragged into the rest of this shit unaware and without any semblance of a say in it."

He snarled into my mind.

When I focused on him through the link, I could feel his chest heaving as he sat on the floor of the boat, his massive legs sprawled out in front of him. Even more than that, I could feel his intense shock at my words.

He genuinely hadn't realized, or didn't believe, what I'd said.

I added, *"My power over whether or not we have sex is the only control I have in this situation, and you took that away from me yesterday when you left me on our bed. So no, I'm not going to get out of the water and talk to you. I'm going to stay here as long as I want. Maybe I'll even get myself off, because at least down here, you can't try to take charge of my body. You started this war, but you won't win it."*

My eyes were stinging when I stopped talking, but I ignored the feeling. I couldn't cry underwater. I *wouldn't* cry underwater.

Porter didn't reply, not that I expected him to. What was he going to do, declare me his yet again and try to force me to the surface of the water?

It wouldn't work.

A few minutes passed, and he didn't get back in the water.

Instead, I felt the boat start to move.

It crossed the lake and stopped at the dock.

I wasn't sure whether to cry or thank him when he didn't

get back in the water or demand anything else from me. So, I didn't do either.

And when I tapped into his mind closely enough to see him sit down next to my bikini, beneath a tree, I finally let out a long breath.

He hadn't won again.

I wasn't going to let him win again.

AFTER THE SUN set and the moon rose, I finally admitted to myself that I was starving, food-wise. And that I needed to feed emotion-wise too.

The second part was a predicament, because I was not going to drink from Porter until I had no other choice. I was used to keeping my magic under wraps when I was hungry, but the kind of hunger that accompanied spending a day and a half pushing my magic into the water around me was a different kind of beast.

My power was going to radiate, pulling everyone nearby toward me no matter how hard I tried to control it. There was no way around it. And Porter would probably think it was another battle in our war.

Maybe it was.

I didn't know.

I was just exhausted, and I didn't want to be the one to accept defeat by doing a walk of shame out of the water.

His mind brushed against mine so gently, I wondered if I'd imagined it for a moment.

"*Izzy?*" he finally asked. It was the first time he'd ever used my nickname. Maybe I should've found it big or important, but it just felt hollow.

"*What?*"

"*I asked Evan to drop some food off at our room. Will you go back with me so we can talk? We clearly have things to figure out, and we need to eat.*"

My anger tried to swell, but I was too tired to tap into it.

And too sad.

"*I don't want to talk,*" I said. "*But I'll eat.*"

"*That's fine.*"

I made my way through the water. Though he'd been the one to ask me to come out, it still felt like accepting defeat.

There was no one around when I got out—and instead of immediately yanking his shirt over my head, Porter stood at the edge of the lake with my bikini in one hand and his shirt in the other. He offered me both, and I eyed him.

After a beat of uncertainty, I decided to lean into the ongoing sex war and took the bikini.

He didn't look away as I pulled it on, but he was quiet, and gave me space.

He didn't comment on my radiating magic as we started

toward the Manor. And he didn't try to convince me to end the war, either.

We walked in silence.

It would've been awkward if it wasn't so insanely tense.

I kept waiting for the other shoe to drop, but Porter seemed strangely calm and laid-back. I had no idea what to think or feel about that.

"Do you want to shift and carry me back?" I asked him, a few minutes down the road. It was a long walk at human speed, and I wanted to get it over with quickly.

"Sure." He stopped long enough to strip. Instead of handing me his clothes, like he had in the past, he left them on the ground. "I'll come back for them," he said, when he noticed me eyeing them.

He shifted, but I looked back at the clothes.

It seemed ridiculous for him to make another trip.

I grabbed the bundle before climbing onto his back and burying my hands in his fur. It was insanely soft. It took a lot of effort to resist running my fingers through it.

The warmth of his body felt ridiculously good against mine as I held on to him. And though I wouldn't have admitted it, something about having him against me just felt *right*.

I SLID off Porter's back and picked the foil-wrapped plates up off the floor in front of our room. He plucked them from my hands before I'd fully straightened, so I grabbed the door and opened it, still holding his clothes against my torso. When he set the food down on the bench at the foot of the bed, I handed his clothes back before slipping into the closet to change.

Everything still reeked of random men, but I hadn't heard another word about it from Porter yet.

My bikini went back in the drawer (it was clean enough), and I pulled on a pair of loose sleep shorts and a bralette. I would've been more comfortable braless and in a cropped tee, but sacrifices had to be made for the sex war to be won.

Boob sacrifices were among the acceptable kinds.

When I emerged, Porter was sitting on the floor with a covered plate of food on his lap. I realized he was waiting for me before he ate, and I sat down closer to him than I genuinely wanted to be.

Though I liked feeling him against me, I wasn't stupid enough to let myself get used to the comfort. Or even really embrace it.

He was going to be a jerk again.

And he was going to walk away again.

I grabbed my plate and unwrapped it, though he still hadn't touched his own, and dug into the food. Steak, potatoes, and steamed veggies were a favorite of the wolves—and a definite win in my book.

"I'm doing everything wrong," Porter said.

The words caught me off guard, but I didn't stop the forkful of potatoes headed straight for my mouth.

"If my mom and sisters were here, they'd kill me. I should be doing everything I can to make this easier for you."

That one made me pause for a moment, but I caught myself quickly and continued eating.

Porter ran a hand through his hair. It was just as messy as usual, but maybe a little more tangled than it often was. "What you said when you were in the lake was right. I'm sorry I've hurt you, and I'm going to do better."

I took another bite of potatoes.

Nope, wasn't acknowledging *that* promise. I didn't believe him. And even if I had believed him, I wasn't going to act any different. He hadn't earned that.

Finally, he unwrapped his plate and started eating too.

Guess we were done talking.

Finally.

IZZY

WE ATE in silence until I finally stood up and made my way to the bathroom wordlessly. I'd pulled the curtain over the doorway a few days earlier, so there was a little more privacy.

The lake water was clean enough that I didn't really *need* to wash my hair, but I wanted to give myself more time before I went back out there and found Porter gone again. So, I showered.

Afterward, I pulled a brush through my hair and put my clothes from earlier back on. Throwing some lotion on my face and brushing my teeth came last, before I padded back into the room.

I stopped suddenly in the doorway, the curtain falling halfway over my shoulder.

I blinked once.

Then again.

Porter was sitting on our bed. His back was propped up against a pillow.

He was typing on his phone, but paused and lifted his gaze to move over my face and down my body for a moment before he looked back at his phone.

He probably just needed to use the bathroom or something.

Letting out a short breath, I finally walked to the bed. My gaze caught on a pile of underwear in the far corner of the room, and I noticed a balled-up sheet beneath it, along with the blankets that had been on the bed.

I'd never seen the sheets and blankets that were on the mattress before, so it seemed safe to assume Porter had stepped out to find them while I was getting ready for bed. Or maybe he'd asked someone else to bring them over.

Either way, he'd definitely gone hunting for the underwear I hid around the room. And found most of it, by the looks of the pile.

He went into the bathroom while I slipped into bed. Though I could've redistributed the underwear to continue the war, I figured my efforts would be best spent in another way that he wouldn't see coming.

And I didn't really want to share my bed with dirty underwear.

So, I just sprawled out in the middle of the bed. I always

slept like that, and since Porter would be leaving, I saw no reason to stop.

Not wanting to watch him walk away from me again, I pressed the button to lower the canopy, and got comfortable in the dark, cozy space.

Maybe I wouldn't feel so lonely that night.

Closing my eyes, I let out a slow breath. Though I could still smell the other men faintly, Porter's scent was much stronger. And more pleasant too. Honestly, it relaxed me.

I wasn't even almost asleep a few minutes later, when the canopy lifted.

Porter rolled underneath it, and I turned my face toward him. My forehead creased, but my heartbeat picked up a little.

There was no way to stop my body from responding.

"What are you doing?" I asked.

"Sleeping next to my mate." He pulled the blankets away just enough to slide beneath them, and I bit the inside of my cheek.

What was I supposed to do?

The sex war would require draping my body over his and driving him as close to insane as possible.

Self-preservation demanded I scoot to the other side to get away from him.

Logic told me there wasn't a chance in hell I'd be able to stop myself from rolling on top of him as soon as I was unconscious. But, most of me wanted to screw logic and lean hard into the self-preservation route.

"Can you scoot over a little?" Porter asked, his gigantic body squished up against one side as he tried not to touch me.

I did what he'd asked, but didn't give him the entire bed.

It was *my* bed.

I needed to hold my ground.

"I haven't slept on a mattress since I lost my family," he said, his attention trained on the canopy above our heads as it descended over us again.

"Seriously?"

"Yeah. Haven't tried sleeping in my human form, either."

My uncertainty faded slowly, giving way to heartache.

The loss had hit him so insanely hard.

"Do you miss them?" I knew the answer to the question before I asked it, but I thought it might get him to open up a little.

"All the time. Do you miss yours?"

My parents.

Someone must've told him what happened to my family. Probably Hale, because I knew Blair had told him the story.

"No." The blunt answer was honest, but Porter's lack of response made me think I'd caught him off guard.

Hale wouldn't have known what my parents were like. Him and Blair hadn't been close for that long. He'd eventually hear all of the stories, but there were undoubtedly some that were still private.

And though my sisters had an idea how things had been for me, none of them knew the full story. Not that I planned to give it to Porter, either.

"You weren't close?" he asked me.

"No. We definitely weren't close."

He moved a little. I got the feeling that he wanted to scoot closer to me, but he didn't actively pull me into his arms. I thought maybe he was trying to be respectful after I yelled at him mentally while I was underwater.

"Are they the reason you keep your magic controlled more than your sisters?" he asked me.

Hale must've told him that too.

Or maybe he'd just picked up on it. It wasn't a stretch, considering that he had only ever felt my power when I wanted him to.

Other than during our walk back to our room. And probably in that very moment.

"They are," I said.

His hand brushed mine, and my throat swelled with the soft, intimate touch.

I pulled it away.

"My sisters were my best friends," he said. "I was the oldest. It was my job to protect them. But we were all so close in age that as they learned how to protect themselves, the responsibility faded out. We did everything together. I considered Hale, Evan, and Bane good friends, but I did everything with Lana and Eve. Our parents too, a lot of the time."

I glanced over at him, and saw him still staring up at the canopy.

"They taught all three of us how to become the alpha, even though we all knew I was the one who'd take the mantle when it became necessary. Lana and Eve could kick ass, but they were softer than me. And an alpha can't be soft. Your sister Clementine reminds me of them. Bright. Cheerful. Smart. Nice."

"I'm not any of those things."

He chuckled. "Like hell you aren't."

"I guess I'm smart," I corrected myself. "Smart enough to know how to win our war, at least. I definitely wouldn't call myself cheerful, though. Definitely not nice."

"You consistently accept presents you don't want from pack members you aren't interested in forming relationships with, because it's the right thing to do. You don't think that's nice?"

"I call that basic human kindness. I would've tried to help them, if I was nice. Clem would've tried to help them."

"My sisters would've, too. Even if it cost them their sanity. You're not soft, Izzy, but that's not a bad thing. I wouldn't have mated with you if were soft. I couldn't survive breaking the woman I tied my life with. I'm not a good man, but I have limits."

"You had already agreed to mate with one of us. It could've easily been Clem."

"I was desperate, but not desperate enough to ruin someone whose personality couldn't survive with mine. I saw the steel in your eyes when we met. I knew you could handle it." He paused. "That doesn't mean you should have to handle the shit I've put you through, though. I should've realized what I was doing sooner."

"You've been in the dark a long time." I didn't want to excuse him, but we both knew it was the truth. "Hale warned me when I agreed to mate with you. They all tried to talk me out of it. I chose this. I'm not going to let you get away with being shitty—but being here was my choice."

"I'm glad it was you."

Somehow, despite everything, I was too.

His hand brushed mine again.

This time, I didn't have the heart to pull away.

He slipped his palm against mine and his fingers between my own. My throat swelled, but my chest warmed.

Maybe I could understand why Blair liked holding Hale's hand after all.

"Is the constant magic a part of your sex war?" he asked me, after a few minutes of silence that felt suspiciously *peaceful*.

Oh.

Right.

"No. Pushing my magic out into the water is just draining. No amount of control can stop me from radiating right now."

"You're hungry?" His grip on my hand tightened slightly. "You should've said something."

"I thought you'd realize."

"I know next to nothing about sirens. I planned on asking Hale for the information when your sisters were here, but I was preoccupied with fighting the urge to drown myself in an attempt to get to you."

My lips curved upward. "Siren magic is a bitch."

"The sexiest bitch," Porter agreed. "You can feed without kissing me. That wouldn't affect the sex war, right?"

"I guess."

"Try it."

"Is that an order?" My voice was upbeat, but there was a warning beneath it.

"A strong suggestion. Fueled by my desire not to let my mate starve."

I rolled my eyes, but focused on his hand and tried to find his emotions.

They hit me immediately.

Comfort.

Uncertainty.

Shreds of hope.

I went deeper, and was surprised when I discovered that the emotions had shifted.

Guilt.

Self-hatred.

Sadness. A lot of sadness.

And below that?

Steely determination.

It was like someone had lit a fire inside him. The darkness of his past still lingered, and definitely didn't look like it was going anywhere. But that determination? It was unlike anything I'd ever felt from him before.

I wanted to ask what he was so determined to do or change, but we weren't there.

We were still at war.

I drank his emotions until I was sated, feeling him light up more as I continued to feed.

When I finally released him, he let out a long breath. "Shit."

"I don't try to hurt you when I drink," I defended myself, starting to pull my hand away.

His fingers tightened on mine. "It didn't hurt that time. I think I'm adjusting to it."

I lifted my eyebrows, but didn't say anything.

What was I supposed to say?

The relief that washed through me eased the tension in my shoulders entirely, though.

"Your magic feels like being injected with life, Izzy. That's the only reason I couldn't handle large amounts of it. I let myself become so used to barely staying alive that it hurt. If not for you, I'd still be in the forest, hiding from the pack."

"Trying to cope isn't the same as hiding."

"Maybe not, but they're similar. I shouldn't have left. And when I heard about Curtis, I should've come back. I was just so angry, I knew I'd end up as bad as him."

"You weren't ready," I said simply.

"I don't know that I'm ready now. My dad would be furious with how little I'm doing in the pack. I'm going to fix that."

"Then I'd say you *are* ready now. There's no reason to hate yourself for the way you grieved. You can't go back. If you could, you still wouldn't have been ready. All you can do now is move on, and try like hell to survive the change."

"The change you survived at what, fourteen?"

"I wasn't an alpha," I pointed out. "And Blair was basically our leader, so I didn't have any real responsibilities other than coming up with some kind of online business to start. On top of that, I was glad my parents were gone. It was nothing like your situation."

"You still had to be strong."

"I just did what I had to to survive, like everyone else." I slipped my hand out of his, and he let me go. "We're still at war, Porter."

"Do your worst, baby."

I rolled onto my side, so I could finally look him in the eyes. "I'm not your baby, remember?"

His lips curved upward slowly. "Not yet."

"Not ever." I brushed a hand over his cock, and felt it harden immediately beneath my touch. He closed his eyes, letting out a harsh breath.

"Fuck me."

"You'll have to beg if you ever want that to happen again."

"I'll put it on the calendar."

I dragged my hand slowly over his length, and he throbbed hard. "Wouldn't take much to get you to the edge, would it? Even with our room smelling like a bunch of other men."

"Don't remind me how much I want them dead."

"Why not?" I slipped my hands into the waistband of his shorts, and earned a low groan when I wrapped my hand around his length.

He seemed to have forgotten the question as I stroked him slowly, watching him move beneath my touch with something that felt a lot like pride. One of his hands slid between my thighs, but his fingers were pointed away from my core. He was just gripping my leg, like it was an anchor or something.

His other hand found my wrist, but he didn't try to stop me as I worked him lightly.

When I released his erection and lifted my hand to his mouth, his eyes met mine for a moment.

And damn, they burned.

I nodded toward his hand, and the bastard knew exactly what I wanted.

He licked my palm slowly, and maintained his grip on my wrist when I wrapped my fingers around his cock again.

His chest rumbled darkly as I stroked him, my hand slick.

His hips rocked.

He gritted his teeth.

I dragged him to the edge—and then stopped while he throbbed, his pleasure fading.

"I shouldn't have done what I did," he growled, while I waited for him to come down from the ledge a second time.

"You think?" I continued, resuming stroking him after giving him a moment's rest.

Somehow, it was one of the hottest experiences of my life.

His fingers dug into my leg as I edged him again, and again, and again, until I knew I'd tortured him longer than he'd done it to me.

Then, I finally released his erection and rolled onto my back again. I could hear his chest heaving as he struggled with the need.

"How long did you feel sick for?" he asked.

"Two or three hours."

"Then you do this every night until you're satisfied with the revenge. Make me hurt."

"No. Once is enough."

"I deserve worse."

"You deserve to move on. So move the fuck on and finally start acting like my mate."

His grip on my thigh tightened. "Alright. I'll move on."

I knew it wasn't going to be that simple.

He must've known that too.

But neither of us brought it up as his breathing slowly

evened out. Or as I reluctantly let myself curl up against his side.

Or as he pulled me half over him, settling the loneliness that had been inside my chest every night I went to sleep without him.

My body seemed set on forgiving him—but I wasn't going to let him off that easily.

He had been suffering, and I hated that for him. But that didn't erase what he'd done.

sixteen

PORTER

I EXPECTED to toss and turn all night.

I hadn't slept through the night since the day I killed my family's murderer. Hell, I hadn't slept more than two or three hours a night since then.

But by some insane miracle, when I woke up with my mate in my arms, it struck me that I'd made it all night.

All night.

I felt better than I could ever remember feeling.

At some point while I was asleep I had rolled onto my side. She'd turned too, so her ass was against my erection and her back was to my chest.

The feel of her body against mine like that was so good, I couldn't stop my arm from tightening around her.

Pulling her closer.

All she had on was those tight shorts and the little bra that didn't hide a thing, so my arm was around her bare abdomen.

I'd never wanted anyone or anything as badly as I wanted her.

And my balls still fucking ached from the night before. I deserved it, though. I screwed up, and I was paying for it.

"You awake?" she murmured.

The sound of sleep in her voice made my cock throb. She rocked her ass against me lightly, and I bit back a groan at the pain of my need. "How long does a sex war have to last?"

"Longer than a day."

"How would one army surrender?"

"I don't know. I'm not the one who started the war."

I hissed as she ground against me harder. "Baby…"

"You finally started using my name right. Let's not move backward."

"Fine." I wrestled the urge to slide my hand into her shorts and see if she was as wet as she smelled. "*Izzy*," I corrected, "Tell me how to surrender."

"I know you didn't just give me another order."

"Never," I gritted out.

She pulled my arm off her waist, and I clenched my jaw when she slid away from me, leaving me hard and throbbing painfully. "Don't take care of that yourself, or I'm redistributing the underwear."

"Wouldn't dream of it."

Her lips curved upward—then she disappeared into the closet.

My jaw clenched tighter when she reemerged in what had to be her tiniest bikini.

I wanted her wrapped around me so bad, it hurt.

"Back to the lake?"

"After breakfast. I'll probably have to stop here to drop off presents again afterward," she said, striding toward the bathroom and disappearing behind the curtain.

I forced myself off the mattress and followed her in. My cock hurt, but I'd just have to deal with that for a few days. Or a few weeks. Until she decided I'd paid enough for being a dick.

I could handle it. I deserved it.

Izzy was braiding one section of her hair when I stepped up behind her. She wasn't French-braiding, just tying it back. I'd heard enough about hair from my sisters to know that it wouldn't last through a swim with how long she spent underwater.

I pulled the hairband off the braid she'd already finished, and earned a sound of protest. When I started a new one at the top of her head, her protests faded, her eyes wide and her lips round.

"You know how to braid?" she asked me.

"I told you I was close with my sisters. Their hair would get tangled with leaves every time we shifted if they didn't braid it. Lana would braid Eve's hair while I braided Lana's. I always ended up with enough leaves in my hair for all three of us."

Her mouth closed.

She watched me with new eyes as I made my way down her head, slowly enough that my sisters would've teased me. The memories hurt, but not as badly as I would've expected.

"It's been a while, so it's not the best," I warned. "But no one else is putting their hands in your hair, so—"

"It's perfect," she said, and there was no sarcasm behind the words.

I finished one braid, and started on the other. She reached back to touch the finished one, and her expression grew more surprised as she felt the smooth, tight strands.

"I'm going to breakfast with you," I said. "Give me a minute to change."

"Alright."

"I'll shift and carry you to the lake afterward."

"Okay."

Her short responses told me she didn't entirely believe me, but that was to be expected. I'd caused it.

I tied the end of the second braid and set my hands on her bare shoulders. "If you really prefer swimming naked, you should do it. Just put your swimsuit under a rock or something and change before you get out. Please."

She eyed me suspiciously through the mirror. "You're acting weird."

"I told you I was going to do better."

"People say that and don't mean it all the time."

"Not me."

She still didn't look like she believed me, but that was what it was. I'd prove myself to her eventually.

WE WERE both ready a few minutes later. I offered her my shirt, or to grab her one of the swimsuit coverups I saw in her closet, but she refused both.

Her sex war just might be the end of whoever stared at her for too long in the cafeteria.

I sent alpha commands into the minds of everyone I caught checking her out for too long, forcing them to look away, as we grabbed our food. The suspicious looks she sent me told me she was picking up on it, but I didn't give a damn. If she wanted a war, she was going to have to deal with the consequences.

I didn't touch my food as she started eating, my attention scanning the room as I watched for anyone who was looking too closely.

Izzy was halfway through her plate when she finally put her hand on my arm. I looked down at her, and she met my gaze as she said into my mind, *"Give me your shirt."*

I blinked.

"We're still at war," she clarified. *"But give me your shirt."*

I peeled it over my head, and she took it, tugging it over hers and slipping her arms through. I relaxed immediately when her torso and ass were covered, and she returned to her food.

Finally, I picked up my fork.

Kim sat down beside Izzy a few minutes later, and Izzy glanced over at her inquisitively when she realized the other woman didn't have any food.

Kim handed her a large tablet. "Our designer sent over a handful of basic ideas for your room," she explained.

Izzy's forehead creased. "Why?"

"You're redecorating," Kim said. She seemed annoyed, but she was the one who had insisted on being involved in all of the alpha stuff so she could spend more time with Evan.

"We are?" Izzy looked at me.

"You are." I took another bite of my food.

"Why?"

"You don't feel comfortable here. I need to change that."

"You wanted to leave the pictures of your family up," she reminded me mentally, to keep the conversation private. *"Every designer would take them down."*

"My mother would be horrified if she knew I made my mate live in a room full of pictures of the people I've lost. My sisters would be, too. It's time for me to accept that this is the life I'm living now."

"That sounds miserable."

"I'm mated to a gorgeous, fiery siren who likes sex enough to start a war over it. I could do a lot worse."

Her face reddened slightly before she turned back to her food, and I couldn't suppress my grin.

I'd made her blush.

I'd make it a goal to do that a lot more in the future.

She looked at the pictures on the tablet with Kim, giving her opinions on everything. Kim took notes on her phone, and sent them to the designer. After they were done, Kim left us to finish up our breakfasts.

After setting a few things into motion for my mate the day before, I'd spent most of my time combing through the pack through the link the way my father had taught me. Doing so had given me a better idea of where I stood with the pack— and it was far from great.

It was time to do better with that, too.

So, after I carried my mate to the lake, I found Evan in my office.

"Ready?" I asked him.

His lips stretched in a twisted grin. "Always."

And we headed out to deal with the first threat together.

seventeen

IZZY

THE NEXT TWO weeks passed quickly.

And strangely.

The sex war technically continued, but Porter didn't fight back. He let me tease him, but didn't really tease me. Didn't try to touch me, either. Without him fueling the fire, my efforts grew half-hearted. I still wore my most revealing clothing and grinded my ass against him now and then, but he didn't comment on it unless he was complimenting me.

He was exhausted when he got to our room every night, but open and playful when he braided my hair every morning.

I would've been concerned about his tiredness, but every time I peeked into his mind, I found him working with Evan. Sometimes, they were talking to or questioning pack members.

Once, I saw him kill someone who had been secretively communicating with one of Curtis's allies outside Mistwood and the pack.

But most of the time, they were working through paperwork and other stuff like that.

Thanks to Blair, I knew that the king's mates were typically expected to help run their kingdom. There was a lot to do, and two people could handle it a lot better than one.

But Porter hadn't asked me to. Or offered me the role. Obviously, I wasn't going to try to take it. So, I wasn't involved.

I spent all of my time in the lake—and honestly started to get bored of it, for the first time in my life.

It was relaxing, but apparently there was such a thing as *too much* relaxation.

Maybe I needed to see if any of the women running businesses in Wolf Manor needed some help or something.

With my mind made up, I got out of the water and pulled my swimsuit on earlier than usual. Porter had picked me up from the lake every day, so I hadn't done the walk back in a while. But I didn't *need* that.

I walked over to my snack basket beneath the tree I always left it at, and grabbed my towel. I'd pulled it over my shoulders and wrapped it around my body before I realized it was slightly damp.

It must've rained while I was in the lake.

It wasn't wet enough not to use it, so I dried my face as much as possible, and quickly did the same with the rest of my body too. I finally looked down at my skin when I pulled the towel off my legs, and horror struck me.

Glitter.

Streaky, uneven glitter.

I immediately lifted the towel to my nose and sniffed.

Chlorine.

Someone had dipped my towel in chlorinated water while I was swimming, and brought it back.

What the hell?

I grabbed my phone out of the basket and opened my camera, watching my eyes widen as I saw the glitter streaked across my face too.

Another look down showed the same over the rest of my body.

Fury rolled through me.

I *hated* glitter, and the streaks of it were even worse than the normal thin layer that would've appeared if I'd simply gone swimming in chlorine.

Was this Porter's fault?

Did he think that was part of the sex war?

Because it *wasn't*.

But if it was his idea… well, he'd definitely won the battle.

My fingers trembled as I pulled up Blair's contact information and hit the button to call her. She answered after it rang a few times.

"Hey, Iz! How's it going?"

"Bad. I need a favor."

"I'm listening."

"Can you chlorinate one of your pools?"

"Sure." There was a pause before she asked, "What happened?"

"A chlorinated towel. I don't know if it was Porter or someone else, but I'm all streaky. And chlorine would probably kill the fish in my lake, so that's not an option."

"I'll add it to the water right now. Will Porter let you leave the pack's land?"

Evan had set up a guard for me that first day, and though he stayed back, he was always there. The only times he left was when Porter ordered everyone to stay away from me.

I'd never tried to escape him, but given my speed, I *could* outrun him if I tried.

And I did remember Evan's map. And his explanation about the path that circled the entire manor. It wasn't that far from the vampire wing to where I was. "I won't give him a choice."

It would probably only work once... but maybe I wasn't as trapped as I'd thought.

"Alright, I'm headed for the pool now. It'll be ready whenever you get here."

"Thank you."

"Of course. This is what sisters are for."

I ended the call and glanced into the forest. I could see the wolf in the trees, watching me. I could've told him what I was doing... but if Porter was responsible for the towel, that bastard could deal with a little worry until he figured out where I was going.

I lifted a hand to wave at the guard—then ran.

GETTING into Vamp Manor was a whole different beast. The guards at the doors weren't thrilled about letting me in, so I had to call Blair back. She had to call them too, before they finally let me through.

Porter's mind touched mine as I stepped through the doors.

"Why am I getting a call from your guard to tell me that you made a run for it?" He sounded strangely calm. I'd expected fury. Then again, he'd calmed down a lot since he promised to do better.

Plus, he could feel my location. He would know without asking that I was with the vampires.

"Probably because I made a run for it."

"You can't win our sex war from Vamp Manor."

"I've already won the sex war. You just haven't surrendered yet."

"I tried to surrender. You refused. Why did you go to the vampires?"

That was true.

And a valid question, from his point of view. Unless he had chlorinated my towel.

I headed down the hallway, toward the elevator that would lead up to Blair's gigantic pool. The thing was a masterpiece. It was at least ten stories high, made of gorgeous stone, with a handful of different tunnels and caves. It could star in any siren's wet dream. Which was why Hale had built it in the first place.

A siren could lure anyone, but to lure a siren? A pool like that was your best bet.

"Did you put chlorine on my towel?" I asked him.

There was another pause. *"Why would I put chlorine on your towel? I'm trying to convince you to give up the war, not piss you off."*

Another valid question.

"That wasn't an answer, Porter."

"No, I did not put chlorine on your towel. Who would do that?"

"I don't know. Maybe someone heard it doesn't react well with siren skin. Have you told anyone about it? And found everyone who wants me dead?"

"I don't think I've mentioned it to anyone, but I'll try to remember if I have. I've been working through the pack

members to weed out anyone disloyal, but there are ways around exposing your thoughts and feelings to the alpha. It'll take time, but I'll find them. Especially if they tried to hurt you."

I let out a slow breath and nodded even though he couldn't see me. Stepping into the elevator, I leaned back against the wall.

It had only been a few weeks since I was there, but it felt like a lifetime.

"I asked Blair to chlorinate her pool. There's no way to get the glitter off, and it'll look a lot worse if it's streaky than if I just take a dive. I would do it on our land, but the chlorine could hurt the fish."

"I didn't know you were that partial to the fish."

My lips curved upward slightly. *"I work hard to maintain a healthy eco system."*

"Your sex war has me so horny, even that somehow turns me on."

I laughed aloud as the doors opened, and I faintly heard my sisters' voices down the hall.

"I think that works in my favor."

"Everything works in your favor if it gets us closer to you letting me surrender, baby."

"I'll think about it."

"I'll take that. And I'll be headed your way as soon as I talk to Hale about it. I trust the vampires, but I don't like knowing there

are walls and security guards that don't answer to me between us."

"Alright. You're going to want to go back to sleeping in the forest after you find me, though. The glitter will get everywhere."

"I like glitter."

"Liar. No one truly likes glitter when they can't scrub it off their skin and out of their hair."

He chuckled. *"I'll like glitter if it's on you. And if it's on both of us, it's just another way to publicly claim you."*

"Good point. We should've tried that from the beginning. Glitter, instead of public sex."

"It would be more fun to combine the two."

I snorted as I reached the wide, open room that housed the pool.

My sisters all looked at me, gathered around the pool and wearing their swimsuits.

"Hey, Iz!" Clementine waved from the poolside.

"I guess we don't need to ask how she is," Zora remarked. "She's grinning like a moron."

"She can hear you," I said.

"She's probably too happy to care, though," Blair said, winking at me before she leaned over the water and dipped her hand in the pool.

When she pulled it out, there was a thick layer of glitter on her skin.

"How much did you add?" Avery asked, eyeing the glitter.

"Too much," Zora grumbled. "I've never seen it that thick."

"It was a happy accident," Clementine said cheerfully. "The fae will love it tonight."

Blair's eyes widened as Clem dove into the water, and she looked at me. "We have a problem, other than your streaky glitter."

"Already?" I strode toward my sisters, hugging all three of them that were still dry.

"I forgot to check my schedule," Blair said, as she hugged me back. "We're supposed to host the fae tonight. Water helps ease the effects of their eclipses somehow. With our magic improving the water, they think it'll make a huge difference"

"What does that mean?"

"I'm not really sure how it works, but the fae realm has been eclipsed for a while. Apparently it makes it difficult for them to fight beastly tendencies. We were going to help them—but they need the water we purified. And I just poured chemicals in it."

"Too many chemicals," Zora added.

"Right." Blair ran a hand over the top of her head. "Shit. I'll have to ask Damian to call Kai's guys."

"We can probably have them use my lake," I said. "I'll need to make sure Porter's okay with it, but I don't see why he wouldn't be."

Her eyes brightened a little. "That would be perfect."

I set my phone on the floor.

"What's the problem?" Clementine asked, as she surfaced. She glittered more than anyone I'd ever seen, and I bit back a groan.

One more living disco ball, coming right up.

I dove in while they explained the situation to Clem, reaching back out to Porter.

He was just hanging up the phone after a conversation with Hale that had, expectedly, gone his way.

"Quick question," I said. *"How opposed are you to loaning my lake to the fae for the night?"*

"My level of opposition would depend on the reasoning behind it. And your level of participation."

I quickly told him about Blair forgetting to check the schedule, and how the water was supposed to help the fae.

"I'd prefer to be there to make sure they're not doing anything to the water that I don't want them to, but if you don't think it's safe, I can stay in our room. It's my fault that Blair chlorinated her pool, though, so I think we should help her. And the fae," I finished.

"I agree. I'll call Hale back, and we'll both talk to Kai. The fae would probably prefer the lake if it's an option anyway, because of the plants."

"Will they kill my fish?" I checked.

"Nah. They'll improve the plants, which will probably make your ecosystem healthier."

"Good to know."

"I'm headed your way, so I'll figure things out and see you soon."

"Thanks, Porter."

"You're welcome, baby."

I snorted underwater at the nickname, but finally gave up on telling him not to call me that. Protesting only seemed to encourage him anyway.

Swimming back to the water's surface, I propped my overly-glittery arms on the edge of the pool. "Porter's going to talk to Hale and Kai. They'll get everything set up to host the fae on the pack's land."

Relief crossed Blair's face. "Thank you."

"This is what sisters are for, remember?" I teased.

She smiled. "How's the water?"

I shimmied my shoulders a bit, so my glitter caught the light. "Sparkly."

Blair laughed, pulling her t-shirt over her head so all she had on was her swimsuit. "Make room."

Clementine and I both scooted over, and Blair dove in. A tiny bit of water splashed on Avery's face, giving her a few glittery speckles, and she smiled.

"Guess I'm joining too."

Her coverup followed Blair's, and she followed our golden-haired sister in, leaving Zora as the lone non-glittery siren.

"Come on, the water's nice," Clementine sang.

Zora rolled her eyes—but took a few running steps before she did a cannonball in, spraying all of us. She swam toward the bottom of the pool with Blair and Avery.

Clem and I laughed as we wiped more water from our faces. "I've never seen this much glitter before," I said, watching my hand catch the light. "It's ridiculous."

"But fun," Clementine said with a smile.

"I guess."

"Think your mate will like the glitter?"

"Probably. Our sex war is driving him crazy enough that I think he'll like it by default."

Her lips stretched in a smile. "Do you like being mated?"

The question caught me off guard. "I haven't really thought about it."

She pulled her long, red hair into a quick bun while I considered it. Clementine had a lot of energy, without a doubt, but she knew when to ease back.

"I'm not sure," I finally said. "At first, it was miserable. He was avoiding me. That hurt, even if I didn't really know him. But the last few weeks have been different. Now it feels like... having a partner. I don't know that I like it, but I don't *dislike* it."

"Hale has gotten a lot of offers from random magical beings since you left. They list out what they could give a siren mate, and how they could protect her. They're trying to arrange a mating, like yours and Porter's," she explained. "The dragon king has sent a lot of them."

My eyebrows lifted. "Seriously?"

Clem nodded, her usual cheerfulness fading a little. "Hale emails them to us. I've looked through them a bunch of times, and thought about it. The way Hale looks at Blair... I want that, you know?"

I nodded, biting my lip.

I'd never felt that way myself, but it didn't surprise me that Clementine did. She had always been a romantic. And while she talked big about sleeping around, I knew she didn't enjoy many of her one-night stands. She was just looking for someone she could stick with.

"I've been talking to Avery about it. If I mated with Talon, the dragon king, I'd be safe. Right? And Blair's told us that he says he needs a siren for something. So I'd be safe, and wanted. Isn't that enough?"

"If you can choose between safe and wanted, and loved, I don't think it is," I admitted.

She let out a long breath. "I know. But how am I supposed to find love when everyone wants something from us?"

"By waiting for the right person?" I suggested. "Other than that, I don't really know."

"That makes two of us."

Blair and Zora surfaced with battle-cries as they hauled ass out of the water, lunging toward the other opening of the pool and diving back in.

"Damn, that's a lot of glitter," I remarked.

Clem laughed, though it was a little half-hearted. "We're going to sparkle for weeks."

"Every siren's dream."

She met my eyes with a smile, but it looked forced.

"What does Avery think about the dragon king?"

"She thinks Talon's insistence that he needs a siren means I should stay as far away from him as possible. There aren't many things a man needs a siren for, and he's not struggling with moving on from his past the way Porter was. As far as we can see, the only reasoning would be problems with his man parts, or some kind of torture."

I snorted. "Magical beings don't get erectile dysfunction."

But unmated sirens *could* be used as a part of a torture process. It hadn't been done since young arranged matings had become a thing for us, but it *had* been done before.

"It's the best possible reason though, isn't it?" Clem teased.

"Honestly, yes."

She laughed, turning around and leaning her head back against the edge of the pool. It didn't look comfortable, but she didn't seem to mind.

"I know an arranged mate bond doesn't come with romance, but part of me wants to just jump in and hope for the best, you know? Hale basically forced Blair to seal the bond with him, and they're so happy together. You should see how much she smiles now. It's ridiculous, and I'm stupidly jealous. Avery keeps telling me that not all arranged bonds end up that way, and I know it's true—but part of me wants to try it anyway."

"My mate bond isn't like that," I said, studying the rock in front of me. "I'm in a sex war, remember?"

"But that's your choice, isn't it?"

"He wasn't sleeping in my bed. It was the best way to force him into it. Much of the time, being mated just feels like one big power struggle."

"But when the power struggle ends, there's happiness, isn't there?"

"I don't know. Is there?" I looked at her, my emotions a bit raw.

Things were looking up for me and Porter, but there was no guarantee he wouldn't step back as soon as I ended our war. There was no way to be sure he wouldn't change his mind about redecorating when the furniture got there in a few days. There was no way to know that he wouldn't get tired of leading the pack like he was, and disappear into the forest.

"I hope so," Clementine said quietly.

"I do too."

As the words slipped out, I realized they were true.

I *did* hope that there was happiness at the end of our power struggle. I *did* want to figure things out with Porter the way Blair and Hale had. I *did* want the kind of love that I'd realized existed.

The kind of love where I could feel safe.

Where I didn't feel alone anymore.

I didn't know how to create it... but I wanted it.

"I'm going to swim with the fae tonight," Clementine said, lifting her voice as she forced cheer back into her tone. Clem was a professional at pretending to be okay until she actually *felt* okay. Or until she managed to convince herself that she did. "I've never been around them much, so I'm excited to see what they're like."

"While glittering like a disco ball? They'll know exactly what you are, Clem. You might as well put a sign on your head that says, 'MATE ME'."

She laughed. "One of Hale's strongest guards agreed to pretend to be my mate for the night. He won't let go of me, so I'll be safe. We were going to draw mate marks on our necks with sharpies. Now, he's the only one who will have to do it." She gestured to the glitter covering her neck. "I can't see your mark at all."

"You're insane," I said, lifting my hand to my throat.

It was weird to think that my mark was completely hidden, but I didn't think Porter would particularly care.

"We said the same thing about you."

Avery broke the water and swam over to us. Her dark hair hung around her face, and she lifted herself up onto the side of the pool to pull it up in a bun on top of her head. "What are we talking about?"

"Clem's dragon king," I said.

Avery sighed. "Please tell me you talked her out of it."

Clementine made a sound of protest, though she was grinning. "She didn't have to. I'm not mating with the dragon king. I want a mate, but I'm not *that* desperate."

"There are so many vampires you could mate with, Clem. If you keep going to the events and game nights, you'll eventually hit it off with one of them," Avery said.

"Theoretically," she agreed.

"You don't sound convinced," I said.

"I'm *not* convinced. I'm tired of being alone."

"Don't we count for anything?" Avery asked.

"Of course you do. But at the end of the day, I don't crawl into bed with you guys. I don't get to have as much hot sex with you as I want—and that was not a suggestion that I want that, by the way. I love you, but having a mate would be different."

She wasn't wrong.

It *was* different.

Because I had a mate, I had a partner that I was stuck with for the rest of my life, for better or worse. It had been for worse, but it *was* getting better.

"If you keep going on dates and meeting new people, it'll happen eventually," Avery promised, taking her hand. "And if it happens with someone who isn't a king, that will be better anyway. No offense, Izzy."

"None taken. There would be much less of a power struggle if you mated with a normal person."

"Alright, fine, I'll keep dating vampires. But I *am* going to swim with the fae tonight. That's not negotiable."

Avery shot me a worried look.

"I'll stay close to her," I promised. "I'm sure Porter will be there, too."

"See?" Clementine gestured to me. "*That's* what I want."

Avery caught her hand and squeezed it. "You'll find it when the time is right."

Personally, I thought she was a little insane for wanting what I had in the moment. But it didn't seem like anything was going to convince her of that, so I didn't bother repeating myself.

Blair and Zora joined us at the surface just as the elevator dinged down the hallway.

Some part of me *knew* that Porter was inside it.

"If you guys are gossiping about us, we'll be forced to drag you into our game," Zora warned, throwing her arms around Clem's shoulders and hanging off her back.

"We would never," Clem said, feigning seriousness.

Zora snorted. "Yeah, right."

"No gossip has occurred," Avery promised, lifting a hand. "Siren's honor."

"We have no honor," Blair said, lifting herself out of the water and plopping down on her ass next to Avery. "Only glitter."

"The glitter is real," I agreed, eyeing my arms reluctantly. It usually took two-ish weeks for all of the glitter to fall off, but I would put my bets on three or four for the insanely-thick layer of glitter we'd collected.

"Did you talk Clem out of going to the fae thing tonight?" Zora checked.

"Nope." Clementine popped her lips on the 'p'. "I'm going. There will be no talking me out of it."

"She's almost as insane as Izzy," Zora grumbled.

"Look at me, I'm fine," I protested.
All of them looked at me, and a few of them stifled laughs.

Maybe the glitter didn't exactly look *fine*.

"I remember you asking us *about clitoral hood piercings*, so I'm thinking *fine* is relative," Clem teased.

"You were asking about *what*?" Porter's voice had me jerking my head back, so I could meet his gaze way behind Blair and Avery.

"I'm out," Zora said, disappearing beneath the water.

"Oops." Clem winked at me before following Zora.

"Good luck," Avery said, flashing me a smile before she dove in after them.

"I'd stay to help, but there's a big, beefy vampire who wants to see my glitter," Blair murmured. "You've got this." She squeezed my shoulder, then used her speed to cross the room in the blink of an eye. She was undoubtedly headed for the elevator.

"It was an idea for the sex war," I explained. "I couldn't go through with it. I'm not quite that brave."

Porter sat down where Avery had been sitting, his lips curving upward as he took in my glitter-crusted face. "Wow."

"I know. It's like someone attacked me with a bedazzler."

"It's cute." He brushed the backs of his knuckles over my cheek, then pulled them away to see how much glitter was on them. There was a grand total of one tiny fleck. "And it doesn't come off easily?"

"Not until it decides to. It's not usually this thick, so it's going to be on for a while. Maybe it will make it easier for you to resist me."

He lifted an eyebrow. "Is your *entire* body covered in glitter?"

"Every inch."

"Then this will make it harder to resist you, not easier. I've never tasted your pleasure while you literally sparkle for me."

"Not *for you*."

"You're my mate. Everything about you is *for me*, even if you refuse to let me have you at the moment."

"I don't think that's—"

He pulled me out of the water and set me on his lap, then kissed me, lightly.

Gently.

Sweetly.

And pulled away long before I was ready for him to. His forehead rested against mine, my eyes closing as our breaths mingled.

"Let me surrender, Izzy."

"No," I whispered, though the last thing I wanted to do was reject him.

There was a reason for my grudge.

I couldn't let it go that easily.

"Why not?" he asked, his lips brushing mine lightly with the question.

"You still have all of the control."

"Tell me how to give it to you, then."

"Let me feed from you whenever I want, instead of according to your schedule."

"Done."

The ease with which he gave in surprised me. I'd never seen him go back on his word, so I didn't have any reason to believe he would do that—but I still couldn't believe he'd give me what I wanted that easily.

"Let me come to Vamp Manor whenever I want to. Don't hold me captive anymore."

He hesitated for a moment with that one.

I could tell he was thinking about it—and probably trying to figure out a way to tell me no.

But he surprised me again by saying, "Alright. But you need to let me know before you leave, and let me come with you."

"That's... fair."

I couldn't imagine Hale letting Blair come to our land without him, so it seemed like a reasonable request for a mated man.

"Warn me, before you claim me in public in any way," I added.

He chuckled roughly. "I learned my lesson about that."

"And don't keep secrets from me, about wolves or about anything else. Mates are supposed to be a team."

"I agree." He lifted his hands to cup my face. "Is there anything else, or can I kiss you now?"

"I want to be able to touch myself without your threat hanging over my head."

"Done. But not without asking if I want to do it myself," he said.

"Is your answer going to be yes?"

"Always." He lowered his mouth to mine. "No clit piercings. I don't want to have to worry about it when I'm rough with you."

My lower body warmed. "You're always rough with me."

"You like it that way."

His lips met mine, and my fingers slid into his hair as he kissed me slowly.

Deeply.

Intimately.

"You taste so fucking good," he said into my mind, tilting my head back to kiss me deeper. *"I missed this."*

"So did I."

He pulled me closer to his chest. *"Tell me the war's over."*

"It's over."

His chest rumbled against mine. The sound was satisfaction, mixed with need. *"I'm taking you home."*

"Agreed."

He kissed me for another minute before he finally released my mouth and stood up. One of his arms was against my back, the other was beneath my knees.

"I don't want to be carried back like a princess," I warned.

"You're not a princess, Izzy. You're a queen." He grabbed my phone off the ground and strode away from the pool. I hadn't said goodbye to my sisters, but I'd text them. They'd get it. The nosy bitches were probably watching quietly from behind a rock, anyway. It's what I would've done if one of them was in my shoes.

"Still."

"You'll ride to the pack land on my back. Until we get out of Vamp Manor, you'll survive being carried like this."

I rolled my eyes at him—but honestly, the way he held me felt amazing.

eighteen

IZZY

BY THE TIME we made it back to Wolf Manor, the fae were already arriving.

That definitely put a damper on our plans.

"I can ask Evan to keep an eye on the lake," Porter said, though he didn't sound convinced. I was on his back, my fingers gripping his fur.

The fae were all walking in a group, and there were at least two or three dozen of them.

"No, you can't. We'll stay there until the fae are gone, and go back to our room together afterward," I said.

"I don't want you swimming with them."

"I don't want to. I don't even know how their magic works. We'll sit on the side of the lake."

He changed directions, heading toward the group, and caught up to them. We got a few curious glances and a handful of waves and nods, but none of them said anything to us.

"Is Kai with them?" I asked.

"No. One of his trusted fae is keeping an eye on them right now. He's in the fae realm. I guess he's trying to figure out why the eclipses keep happening."

"At least we don't have to deal with that."

"No kidding."

The fae all dove into the water as soon as we reached the lake, and none of them bothered staying on the shore. Porter shifted in the forest and pulled on the jeans I'd carried for him, handing me his shirt.

I put it on while he grabbed the chair he'd left when my sisters visited, and he set it up near the place I'd left my chlorinated towel.

The towel was gone, which meant someone had come back for it. Probably either one of Porter's people, or the person who had chlorinated it.

Porter sat down on the chair and pulled me onto his lap. I wasn't sure I'd ever feel *comfortable* with his erection pinned beneath my ass, but it did feel nice.

"If chlorine actually hurt me, today could've been bad," I murmured into Porter's mind while we watched the fae swim around. They were quiet, and peaceful. I needed to let

Clem know that she wouldn't be missing much if she stayed home.

His arm around me tightened a little. *"I know. I have Evan and a few other people trying to figure out who was responsible. We don't have any cameras set up around the lake, but that will change."*

I didn't want to put cameras there, but if we couldn't find the culprit, what was the alternative?

I wouldn't risk my life for a little more privacy. We could always take them down after we figured out who was behind it.

Pulling my phone from my pocket, I took a quick video of the fae and sent it to Clementine.

ME

You're not missing much

Not worth risking your life over

CLEM

Damn

I thought they'd be a little wilder

ME

If you want wild, run with the wolves

Clem

I'll think about it

ME

Sorry

I know you were hopeful about the fae

CLEM

It's fine

I should just go on a date with another vampire anyway

I do love the vamps

ME

They're pretty safe to love

CLEM

Yeah

Thanks for the video, I would've been disappointed

The kings' Christmas Eve party is only a few months away. I'm sure I'll meet some fae then, without the glitter making me a target

ME

I didn't know that was a thing

CLEM

It's a masquerade ball

Cheesy, but fun

Me and Zora are already planning our outfits

I'll plan yours too ;)

ME

LOL

Plan one for Porter too

CLEM

Yessss

It'll be glorious

ME

I don't want him naked

CLEM

You're probably the only mated woman on the planet who feels that way

Porter snorted, and I realized he'd been reading over my shoulder. It probably should've annoyed me, but I would've done the same if he was texting while I was sitting on his lap.

ME

Probably

Love you

CLEM

Love you too

I'm thinking you should do a red riding hood costume, and he can be the big bad wolf ;) I'll make it happen

Have fun with your man!

I grinned at her idea and liked her message, then put my phone in the camping chair's cupholder and murmured to Porter, "How long do you think the fae are going to stay here?"

"All night." His hands slipped beneath the bottom hem of my shirt and slowly stroked my skin. "They seem pretty laid-back."

"They do, but that could change."

"It could." He adjusted the angle of my ass over his erection, and I closed my eyes at the perfect pressure. "If I could touch you without drawing attention, I'd already have you wrapped around my fingers."

My body throbbed. "You've never had me wrapped around your fingers, Porter."

Not physically, or metaphorically.

He chuckled, his chest rumbling against my back. "Only in my imagination."

"You don't want me to follow your commands. If I listened to you, we would never be together like this. You'd still be in the forest."

"You're right. I don't want a good little mate." He nipped at my throat. "I want you."

His mind collided with mine, and his memory of the way I'd moved as he went down on me in the gazebo played out in my mind.

My breathing grew shallower.

He stroked my inner thigh lightly, with his thumb. I wanted more—but the fae weren't far from us. And we'd done the public sex thing, but not *that* public. Porter was too possessive to be okay with that. And I was too.

The memory grew hotter as he bent me over that chair and thrust into me.

I took his emotions in, just a little, and *felt* his pleasure with the memories.

I could almost feel his fingers tracing the spot between us, where our bodies had been locked together.

His memory shifted to the day on the beach, when I'd climbed on his lap.

I sucked in a breath at the way he remembered, in great depth, how he'd torn my bathing suit and filled me.

His thoughts and memories played through my mind as time passed—until a large wolf shifter plopped down on the dirt next to our chair.

I gasped, but Porter didn't seem surprised.

He probably heard or smelled Evan coming.

When the blond man didn't bring up the smell of my desire, or tease us about what we were doing, I looked over at him.

His expression was closed off, his gaze focused on the lake even though I got the impression he wasn't really seeing anything.

"What happened?" Porter asked him.

"Kim." Evan ran a hand through his hair.

Porter waited.

I did too.

"There were things we didn't agree on when Curtis was the alpha. Things we've never agreed on. Big things. Kids. Timing. Family stuff. Her brother." He ran his hand through his hair again. "She sprang this stupid fucking mark on me without warning a few months ago. Made me feel like shit when I wasn't ready to seal the bond. Since you guys took over, it's gotten worse. I can never do anything right with her. Seems like all we ever do is argue."

My horniness deflated, replaced with empathy. "I'm sorry."

Porter set a hand on his shoulder. "If you need to spend less time with the pack, you know I'll make it work."

"I know, but that's the only time I'm ever appreciated. I love working with the pack. She doesn't understand. She doesn't fucking care." He swiped at his eyes. "I can keep an eye on the fae. Go enjoy your night. Someone should."

I didn't want to budge, but Porter squeezed his shoulder. "You're a good guy, Ev. Don't let anyone make you question that. No one has done as much for this pack as you have in the last few decades."

He nodded slowly, and I saw the emotions raging across his face.

"Are you sure you're okay?" I asked.

"I'm sure." He flashed me a grin that didn't meet his eyes. "Get out of here."

Porter chuckled, lifting me with him as he stood up.

Shifting forms, he carried me back toward the Manor.

"Do you think he's really okay?" I asked Porter.

"I think they've been together for so long that if he was ever going to be ready to commit to her, it would've happened by now," Porter said. *"And I think they both know they haven't been*

happy together for a long time, and they either have to figure out a way to fix that, or split up. I've never seen them together when they haven't had more issues than not."

"Damn."

"Yeah. All wolves feel an urge to take a mate from puberty and on, so whatever they decide, it won't be easy to let go. Their animal sides likely see each other as mates, even without the true commitment. I hope they work it out without too much drama."

"No kidding. What about her brother?"

"He broke away from the pack a few days ago, finally, so he shouldn't be a concern anymore. He hasn't been on the pack's land. She sided with us against him when everything happened, so I'm not concerned about that," he explained.

"At least that's one less problem to deal with."

He made a noise of agreement.

We finally reached our room, and I landed smoothly on my feet, typing in the code as Porter stepped up behind me. His hands were on my hips, his thumbs dragging smoothly over my skin.

He turned me so my back hit the door as soon as it was closed behind us, and suddenly, we were alone.

As strange as it was, we'd never had sex in private.

We'd gotten close a few times.

But we had never actually gone all the way in the privacy of our own room.

Porter slowly lifted my hands above my head, pinning my wrists in place as he kissed me. His other hand found my core as I tilted my head back, letting him in deeper. I sucked in a breath as he dragged his fingers over my clit through my swimsuit.

"You're still soaked for me, baby."

"You were playing our sex life through my mind like it was a movie. Of course I'm wet after—ohh."

I couldn't stop my soft groan when he pushed his hand beneath my swim bottoms, and his rough fingers finally brushed through my hot folds.

All words vanished from my mind.

My body rocked, throbbed, and trembled as he continued to touch me.

Part of me was afraid he'd pull away, like he had the last time. That he'd take revenge on me for when I'd done the same.

But he didn't.

And I was crying out with pleasure, my body shaking with the intensity of my release, what felt like only seconds later.

He continued stroking my clit through my climax, murmuring when I came down from the high, "You're so fucking hot."

"I thought you wanted to screw me," I panted, my chest rising and falling rapidly.

"I'm going to. I just want to watch you come a few times, first."

"Why?"

"A man should be able to picture, in vivid detail, the way his female looks when she climaxes. I can't yet."

"Who told you that?"

"It's common sense, baby." He slid a thick finger inside me as he continued teasing my clit. My lips parted, my head falling back against the door as my eyes shut. "Open your eyes. I want you to see whose fingers you're riding."

"I don't think I could forget if I tried."

"If you don't *know*, I'm doing it wrong."

My lips curved a little—until they parted again as he found my g-spot.

My hips jerked.

I fought his grip on my wrists, and he let go. My hands found his shoulders, my fingers digging into his skin as he brought me back to the edge.

In minutes, he had me shattering again, with another desperate cry.

"Porter," I moaned, all of my weight against the door. "I can't—"

"You can." He slid his hand out of me, then wrapped his arm around my backside and hauled me off my feet.

My back was on the mattress a moment later, my ass and legs hanging off the ledge as he kneeled between my legs. I propped myself up on my forearms in time to see him peel my swimsuit bottoms down my thighs.

Neither of us watched the fabric hit the floor.

Leaning in, he dragged his tongue over my core so slowly, it made me cry out.

"Take your top off," he said, the words a clear command.

One I wanted to follow.

Badly.

I sat up long enough to pull the sporty bikini top over my head, and he made a sound of appreciation as my breasts fell free.

Porter released my thigh long enough to grab a pillow, and tucked it behind my back to prop me up higher.

"Play with your nipples for me, baby."

My hands cupped my tits, and I dragged my thumbs over the sensitive points, making him growl. "Now tell me you're mine."

"You know I am."

"I want you to say it." He licked my clit again, torturously slow, and I swore as my hips lifted from the bed.

"I'm yours, Porter."

"You taste like it, too." He nipped at my clit, and I cursed again, arching harder.

He licked and tasted me until I'd unraveled on his mouth once, and again—and then, he leaned over me on the bed.

He was so big, he made me feel small.

The head of his cock pressed against my entrance, and he held one of my thighs in one hand while he held his weight up over me with the other.

We'd never been in that position before.

It was intimate.

Warm.

Real.

My chest rose and fell quickly. "Are you mine, too?" I asked him, and his lips stretched in a slow, sexy smile.

"Entirely, baby."

He lifted my hips higher, and thrust into me.

We moved together as he fucked me, slow, smooth, and deep.

His knot swelled inside me as we lost control together, locking us in that process of need and pleasure until we were both so drained that all we could do was collapse on the mattress.

Porter rolled me on top of him, his cock still buried inside me as his knot softened, but neither of us was in a hurry to end the connection.

"You are the best thing that's ever happened to me, Izzy," he murmured into my ear, as we caught our breath together.

My eyes widened, my heart still pounding hard from the intensity of our releases.

What was I supposed to say to that?

To him?

After we'd wrestled for power so much, after he'd controlled me, after I basically tortured him with our sex war…

What the hell was the right response?

"You don't need to feel the same way, and you don't need to answer." He kissed the top of my head in a way that made my heart basically burn. "But you deserve to know that you're the reason I'm not hiding in the forest anymore. You saved my life when you agreed to mate with me. So thank you."

"I did it for me," I said. "Don't thank me for that."

"You didn't leave."

"You wouldn't have let me go."

"I assigned you a guard who couldn't have stopped you from running away if you tried. I wouldn't have declared war on Hale if you'd hidden with him after you left me. You could've gotten away at any time—you just chose not to."

"It wouldn't have done any good. You would've come after me."

"I would've. But you didn't *want* me to let you go."

The words hit me, hard.

He was right.

I didn't want him to let me go. I never had.

What that said about me, I didn't really want to know.

"What does that mean for us?" I asked him, my heart still beating hard.

"The same thing it's always meant. We're mates. For better or worse." He pulled me against his chest a little tighter.

"I don't know how to be anyone's mate, Porter. My parents were…" I let out a harsh breath. "They weren't good people. They weren't nice. Not to me. Not to each other."

"You know how to be a good sister. I've seen how you are with them. It's not much different to be a good mate—you just add in a little bit of sex."

A choked laugh escaped me. "A little bit?"

"A lot. A lot of sex."

"I don't think it's the same. The way Blair is with Hale isn't the way we all are together. They're like… best friends."

"That's a more accurate way to describe a healthy mated pair. Two people, against the world."

"It sounds nice, but I don't know how to make it happen."

"You don't have to *make* it happen. You just have to *let* it happen."

"Well I don't know how to do that, either."

He chuckled. "I'll handle it."

"I don't like letting you have all the control, remember?"

"I remember. But this isn't about control. It's about fun. Talking. Shared experiences."

That did sound like friendship.

I supposed I did all of those things with my sisters, too.

"You and I have talked a little," I said.

"We're getting there with that," he agreed.

"And we've done a few things together. Like... screwing next to the lake. And in front of your pack."

"Don't forget the sex war. And snuggling every night, over the past two weeks."

"Right."

"We have breakfast every morning, too."

"And you braid my hair."

"Mmhm."

"So we don't have *nothing*," I decided.

"We have a solid mate bond. We just need to work on it a little harder."

"And you want to do that?" I checked.

"More than anything." He kissed my head again. "But first, I want to screw you again."

I sighed dramatically. "You act like we haven't had sex in weeks."

He snorted, and I couldn't stop myself from laughing as he thrusted into me with a grin.

Maybe we had a *lot* more than nothing, but we'd both been too stubborn to admit it.

WE BARELY SLEPT AT ALL, but both of us were grinning as we made our way down the hall to breakfast, our fingers intertwined and our shoulders pressed together.

Izzy's smile faded slightly when we stepped into the cafeteria and received a large number of shocked stares, so I leaned over and murmured, "They're staring because you're covered in glitter, not because you're holding my hand."

"Maybe they're staring because *you're* covered in glitter," she whispered back, her grin returning. She'd tried to scrub the sparkles off both of us, but they hadn't budged. I had far less than her, though all the time we spent naked together had ensured that I did, in fact, sparkle.

"Let them." I squeezed her hand lightly, and she bumped my shoulder. I looked out at the pack—or the part of it that was in the cafeteria at the moment, and announced aloud and through the pack's bond, "My mate and I are going for a run tonight. Anyone who wants to come is welcome."

I felt the immediate change in energy, and my grin widened.

It felt good to be back.

I'd always miss my family—but they would've wanted me to live. And to make sure the pack was doing the same.

So that was what I'd do, for the rest of my life.

twenty

IZZY

PORTER TOOK me to his office after breakfast, and sat me on his lap.

"What are we doing in here?" I asked him, looking over my shoulder curiously.

"Working. We're mates, remember?"

"I don't have a job."

"Sure you do. The alpha female runs the pack just as much as the alpha male does. I'll make a list of all the stuff my mom used to handle, and you can pick and choose what you want to do from it."

"You really want me to help lead the pack?" I asked, nerves setting in a little. "I'm not a wolf."

"The pack is a family, not just a group of wolves. We've got other kinds of shifters here too. Poodles. Cats. Squirrels.

Bears. No one cares if you don't howl at the moon. They care that you're part of the family. Got it?"

"Got it," I agreed, though I was still a little hesitant.

"I'll have another desk put in here. Until then, there's one easy thing you can do as my mate."

"How easy?"

I looked over my shoulder again, and found him wearing a wicked smile. "Very." He lifted me up, bending me over the desk as he pulled my pants down.

I laughed—then moaned when he filled me.

Maybe we weren't going to get a lot done, but we'd have a damn good time.

When we finally separated, we really did focus on work. I sat on his lap for the required after-sex snuggling while Porter explained the basics of what my role required, and I took a ton of notes.

After a short lunch break, we went back to work.

And honestly?

It felt good to have a purpose again.

...other than my ridiculous war.

THAT NIGHT, we gathered with the pack for another bonfire.

It was just as big as the first one I'd attended, but the energy was completely different.

Porter held my hand as we walked around, chatting with people I vaguely remembered. He knew almost all of them by name, and I knew some.

When he asked about their families and brought up their pasts, they lit up in ways I never would've imagined. They all thanked me for bringing him back, but they loved him.

His family had clearly been good leaders.

When we had a brief break from the crowds, we ate s'mores with little kids who didn't know him, chatting with some that were excited to meet him, and giving space to the ones who wanted space.

I loved watching him with the kids.

I hadn't interacted with them much, but I had always liked little kids. Part of me had dreamed about having a big family some day, if I ever ended up safe and mated. I'd never told my sisters that, because I didn't want to see the pity in their eyes.

But now that it was a possibility, it was something to think about.

Porter was pulled into a conversation with some of his closest wolves, and I noticed Evan among them, talking vibrantly.

My gaze caught on Kim, on the other side of the fire. I noticed her watching Evan and Porter, her jaw set tightly.

For hers and Evan's sake, I hoped they could work it out and find a way to be happy together.

My thoughts were interrupted by another pack member who wanted to talk, and I greeted her with a smile.

It was Nora, my favorite (and only) chocolate supplier. She was practically beaming through the whole conversation as she told me about a new hobby she'd taken up now that Curtis was gone. Crocheting.

She promised to bring me a hat and scarf she was making soon. The woman was an absolute sweetheart, and I decided I should figure out a way to hang out with her or something. We needed to be friends.

Before she walked away, she winked and let me know that she had already put in another order for more siren chocolate.

The pack's excitement built up throughout the bonfire until Porter and I stood near the edge of the forest after darkness had set in. He announced in a loud voice that the Mistwood Pack and its new alphas were finally going to run as one—and everyone howled so loudly in response that I couldn't help but grin.

I wasn't a wolf, but I could feel the pack's excitement through the bond anyway.

Porter stepped into the trees and shifted forms. When he emerged a moment later, I slipped onto his back, and he took off into the forest.

He'd carried me in his wolf form so many times before, but never like this.

He ran hard and fast. Wind blew through my hair, whipping my braids around behind me as I held on tightly. I could feel the other wolves behind us—so many of them.

With them at our sides, we weren't just a mated pair. We weren't just Izzy and Porter. We were a *pack*. A group. A family.

My eyes stung as the realization set in.

I was a part of them.

I didn't have fur, but that didn't matter. I belonged there. And I always would.

The group split up as everyone headed off to do their own thing soon enough, but I could feel Porter's joy as he carried me through the trees.

He had no desire to stop.

And I wouldn't ask him to.

He belonged in the forest, just as much as I belonged in the water. Maybe even more.

So I held on as he ran until he'd had his fill of the forest. And when we got back to our room, I *held on* as he bent me over our bed and fucked me hard.

Maybe I did know how I felt about being mated.

Maybe mating with a wolf was the best decision I'd ever made.

. . .

THE NEXT DAY, Porter took me hiking in our human forms. I'd never gone before, but discovered pretty quickly that I enjoyed it.

Especially because I was faster than him in that form.

Though he always dragged me back into his arms when he caught me, we had fun together. A lot of fun.

The day after that, we got in his shitty old truck, and drove into the main part of Mistwood for dinner and a movie.

It was strange to feel like a real couple. Even more strange not to have to hide when I was out in public. But I liked it.

I really, really liked it.

We worked together every day, and every day, he planned something else for us to do after we were done.

A massive game of tag in the forest, with the pack. *Everyone stayed in their human forms, until he cheated so he could take me down.*

Swimming and ice cream with my sisters, in Vamp Manor. *We saw one of the vampires whose underwear I hid in our room, and I had to distract him with my mouth before the guy was murdered.*

Strip poker and dessert, in our room. *I was the dessert.*

Fishing, on my lake. *We released the fish, but I still felt guilty for catching them.*

Swimming with the fae, who kept coming back to our lake on the days their eclipses hit. More of them came every time, and the swims started to look more like parties. More wolves started joining in too, which made the magic fiercer. *We screwed in the water once. Or twice. I was sworn to secrecy.*

Every day, Porter's eyes got brighter.

His grin lasted longer.

The tension in his shoulders eased a little more.

The man was clearly made for fun and adventure. He'd just forgotten it when he lost his family. Grief could do that to a person.

WEEKS WENT BY QUICKLY.

All of my glitter finally came off, and we washed all of our bedding to be rid of it for good.

We spent Halloween passing out candy to the pack's kids, laughing and smiling at their costumes.

They were so adorable, it made my chest hurt.

There had been no sign of the people who wanted me dead. Though we hoped they'd changed their minds, Porter and his top wolves were keeping a close eye on me and the rest of the pack. More cameras had gone up, everywhere.

It didn't seem reasonable that everyone who still disliked me could realize they loved me, so none of us were hopeful for that. But there was nothing we could do to make those people come forward.

So, we just settled into life.

I knew he didn't tell anyone but me about his daily plans for us until after they'd happened, though. It was a way to keep me safe.

We could never be truly comfortable with the threat hanging over our heads, but I hoped we would get there.

A FEW DAYS BEFORE THANKSGIVING, Porter

had to leave our office halfway through the afternoon to meet up with a few of his guys, who thought they'd found a lead. I stayed in the office, determined to finish what I was doing.

Kim came by randomly with a delivery of siren chocolates from Nora. She'd been distant since her fight with Evan, so I asked her how things were going.

She didn't seem like she wanted to talk, just giving me a few short answers about how they were still together before slipping away. It was weird, but not out of character for her at the moment.

I had my way with one of the chocolate bars as I returned to the work I'd been finishing up. I couldn't focus very well, which was frustrating.

But, I chalked that up to nerves about what Porter would find.

Eventually, I gave up trying to finish and reached out to him mentally.

"I'm not feeling my best, so I'm heading back to our room," I told him. *"No rush. Don't worry about me."*

He always worried. My words wouldn't stop that, but I had to say it anyway.

"I'll be there soon. The lead was a bust," he said. *"We can skip our plans tonight and watch a movie in bed."*

"Sounds nice. Will there be food?"

"Of course. I'll bring you dinner, but I'm not hungry for anything but you."

I snorted inwardly. *"Smooth."*

He laughed. *"Always. See you soon."*

His mind left mine, refocusing on whatever he was doing.

I felt a bit woozy as I slipped down the hallway.

I wasn't sure why.

I'd eaten plenty of food, and fed on Porter recently enough that hunger couldn't have been the cause.

My implant made me positive that pregnancy wasn't an option.

Magical beings didn't really get sick, so that was off the table. Maybe I'd eaten some old food or something?

I stumbled a little, and had to stop for a moment. Putting a hand on the wall, I took a few slow breaths as everything around me spun.

"Are you okay?" someone asked me. I recognized Kim's voice immediately, and relief rolled through me.

"Mmhm," I managed.

"We should tell the alpha. Did you talk to him?" Kim asked.

"Just to tell him I'm going to our room." It was a struggle to get the words out.

I tried to reach Porter mentally again, but my mind was such a mess, I couldn't seem to connect with the pack's link.

What the hell was wrong with me?

"Here, I'll help you back to your room," she said, pulling one of my arms over her shoulders. She wrapped her arm around my waist, too. When she started down the hallway, all I could manage to do was try to keep myself on my feet.

"You'll be fine," the woman said, her voice upbeat.

How did she know I'd be fine?

How did she even know what was wrong with me?

I tried to pull away from her, but she was the one carrying my weight, and she tightened her grip when I tried to get away.

"It's just a little wolfsbane, to suppress the mental link," she added. "It doesn't do any permanent damage. It'll bleed out of your system easily enough. Be glad you're not a wolf; you'd be vomiting like mad right now."

I *felt* like I could've been *vomiting like mad*, so her words didn't calm my fears in the slightest.

It seemed like I'd found the person responsible for the chlorinated towel. And now the wolfsbane, apparently.

But why would Kim do that to me?

She was fighting with Evan, but that didn't have anything to do with me. He and I were friends, but we weren't close. I was mated, so there wasn't a chance in hell he had feelings for me.

She towed me down the hallway. I didn't bother trying to tap into my speed. I couldn't see the walls around me well enough not to collide with one, and a broken nose on top of whatever was already happening seemed like a bad call.

"Where are you taking me?" I asked, when I smelled tires and oil.

We had to be in the pack's parking garage. I'd been there a few times—it was under Wolf Manor.

"Away."

Shit.

That wasn't good.

She opened the door of a white SUV, and eased me inside.

If she wanted me dead, I assumed she would've been more violent.

I leaned hard against the door after she shut it, closing my eyes as I waited for my head to stop spinning.

It didn't.

When I tried to open my eyes again, everything was blurry.

She started the car, and I finally passed out when she backed out of the parking space.

twenty-one

IZZY

I WAS SWEATY, trembling, and insanely nauseous when I came to. My heart pounded in my head, and my entire body ached.

My mind went back to the hallway immediately, and I tried to reach out to Porter, but I couldn't feel the pack's link at all.

The poison might've knocked out the pack link, but it couldn't touch our mate bond. He would know exactly where I was, which meant he was coming for me.

I just had to survive until then.

And considering he hadn't found me yet, it seemed safe to assume I hadn't been unconscious for long. That was good.

I felt my stomach start to churn, and immediately rolled to my side. I moved just in time to vomit all over the floor.

When I opened my eyes, I looked around the room, trying to figure out where I was. I was a lot less dizzy than I'd been before I passed out, so that was good.

The space was large for a bedroom, with walls that were covered in brown paneling and a walk-in closet whose door stood open. The darker wood flooring was weathered and scratched. It was nearly black in a crisp rectangle where I was laying, which made me think there had been a bed there for a long time while the sun shone through the wall of windows to my right.

"Disgusting," a male voice growled, barely glancing over at me from behind his computer. The desk he occupied was elegant and oversized.

I partially expected to find Evan there, wondering if he would've betrayed Porter alongside his fiancée, but the guy beside me wasn't Evan.

He actually looked a lot like Kim.

Shit, was that her brother?

The one who hated Porter and had let his own fiancée die without standing up for her?

"If you're going to kill me, just get it over with." I wiped my mouth with the back of my hand. It tasted foul, but there was no water nearby for me to rinse with.

The guy ignored me.

I heard the sound of a message being sent, and a minute later, Kim stepped into the room.

Her nose wrinkled when she saw the vomit on the floor, but she focused on her brother. "Ready?"

"Yeah. Are you guys?" he checked.

"All set. Grab the siren."

The siren.

I'd thought Kim and I were friends, but apparently I'd been wrong.

That stung.

Kim's brother grabbed my waist, and I almost vomited again when he threw me over his shoulder. Porter had done the same thing in the past, but he was gentle. It had been comfortable.

Kim's brother didn't give a damn if it hurt me, and it did. The way my ribs slammed into him made me confident I'd be bruised afterward.

And I had to believe there would be an *afterward*.

They wouldn't have bothered to abduct me if they just wanted me dead. Right?

I lifted my head just enough to try to see where I was going.

He carried me out of the nearly-empty bedroom and into a gigantic living area. There was a wooden chair set up in the middle, and all of the other furniture seemed to have been pushed up against the walls. I was still too dizzy to make out the details from so far away, but the basic shapes were there.

Kim's brother slammed me into the wooden chair hard enough that I saw stars. The wood cracked a little, but thankfully held its shape.

There were four other people in the room. I vaguely recognized one of them, but the others were strangers to me.

Kim's brother fastened me to the chair with zip ties, as if they hadn't already drugged the shit out of me. He pulled them tighter than he needed to, but I didn't give him the pleasure of wincing.

Even though I definitely wanted to.

I reached for the pack's link again. Though I could finally feel it, it was so faint that I couldn't use it or hear anything through it. When I tried to find Porter that way, it didn't work.

I'd need more time.

I focused on the other people in the room—and my eyes widened when I realized that three of the four held guns.

All of which were pointed at me.

The fourth was typing something into a computer.

Kim's brother stepped behind me, and I felt the bite of something sharp. I didn't look down, but it seemed safe to assume it was a knife.

Shit.

Maybe they were going to kill me after all.

"Security cameras finally caught him on the west side of the property," the woman at the laptop said, focusing on her screen as her fingers flew across the keyboard. "Moving as fast as expected

"He's alone, right?" Kim demanded.

"Let me try to zoom in..." the woman continued typing.

"He always worked alone before," Kim's brother said calmly. "I'm sure Evan isn't with him."

Kim nodded, though it looked forced.

She was worried about Evan being with Porter?

Why?

"I don't see anyone else," the woman at the laptop said. "But they could be behind him. We didn't make it into the city's security cameras like we hoped."

"Fuck," Kim hissed. "If Evan's with him..."

"We go through with the plan," the laptop woman said without looking away from the screen. "He'll forgive you after he's alpha."

Wait...

Was she saying Kim *wasn't* working with Evan? She was going against her fiancé?

And wanted to make him the alpha?

Damn.

"Evan and I are friends. If you kill me or Porter, he'll refuse to step up as alpha. He might even kill you," I said quietly, tapping into my magic a little. Though I didn't want to risk pissing anyone off, I had to do *something* to save myself and my mate. My mother had taught me how to slip my power into my voice, to influence a conversation to go my way. I never used it, on principle—but in this situation, I'd dig into every tool I had.

"I'm going to be his mate," Kim said fiercely. "He'll take my side."

"If he killed *your* brother, would *you* take his side?" I asked, pushing a little more magic forward.

"Shut up," her brother snarled, pressing the knife harder into my skin and drawing a small amount of blood.

Kim didn't seem stable—but her brother seemed fucked up.

I backed off on my magic.

Guess Porter was going to have to get us out of the situation on his own.

"Easy, Corbin," one of the guys holding a gun warned Kim's brother. "If he smells her blood, he'll be a lot harder to negotiate with."

The guy had a point.

Corbin, Kim's brother, scoffed.

He moved his knife long enough to wipe at my throat roughly with his sleeve. I winced, but at the same time, was kind of glad he'd have my blood on him.

It would tell Porter who to kill.

The grimace on the other guy's face told me Corbin had only managed to smear the blood over more of my skin.

"It's going to be a miracle if we make it out of this alive," one of the other guys muttered.

Corbin snarled at him, too.

"There's another vehicle incoming," the laptop chick warned. "East side. Driver looks like…"

She trailed off, and all of us looked at her laptop's screen.

"Fuck!" Kim cried out, looking at the door. "I knew this was a bad idea."

"It was *your* idea," the laptop girl tossed back.

"It was Corbin's," she argued.

"You poisoned the chocolate. Only way out now is by killing his mate and making a run for it," Corbin growled.

"He'll still scent her in the room. There *is* no way out now," the laptop girl said, still typing furiously. "I'm closing the east gates. Might buy us a few minutes without Evan."

"He'll scent you in the room too," Corbin told his sister. "You're just as fucked as I am."

"Unless we kill Porter while we distract Evan." Kim's eyes were on me.

Her desperation was definitely showing.

"No. If we kill Porter, the pack kills us," one of the gun guys said, shaking his head. "That was never the plan."

"We took his mate. There's a damn good chance he kills us before they get to," another gun guy said.

"That's what the weapons are for," Kim shot back.

"Everyone, just—" the third gun man began.

He cut himself off when the front door near us swung open, and Porter stepped inside.

His fists were clenched, and the situation was dire, but I was still relieved to see him alive and whole.

His gaze met mine immediately, but he didn't relax.

There was a knife to my throat, after all.

"Hands in the air," Corbin growled. "Step any closer, and she dies."

A vein in Porter's throat pulsed.

He slowly lifted his hands, forcing his fists open.

"Tell your team to turn around," Kim ordered. "We can see them on the cameras, and we don't want them involved."

It was a good idea, actually. Not for me—it was terrible for me. But for them, it was good.

And it wasn't surprising she didn't want Evan involved.

But with the pack link between them, I was sure that Porter had already told Evan exactly who had betrayed them.

I pushed against the mental bond again, and fought to hide my thrill when I finally felt the faintest of brushes.

Porter's mind was against mine, trying to gain entry.

"Lower your weapons," Porter said, his voice authoritative enough that one of the guys actually did lower his gun. "If you leave now, I'll let you live."

The guy who lowered his gun avoided everyone else's gaze and hurried out the door, behind Porter.

My mate didn't look back.

He didn't look away from me at all.

"Give me your terms," he said.

"Release the pack's link to Evan. Step down as alpha," Kim said.

Porter didn't respond right away.

His mind brushed mine, and I faintly heard his voice in my mind. *"Can you access your magic?"*

I tried to respond, but couldn't.

"If you can, send a small amount of it through the room. We want them to lose control without realizing what you're doing. Slowly increase the amount," Porter added.

I did as he'd instructed.

"Evan is a strong wolf, but he couldn't take down Curtis. And Curt's friends are still out there. If I give the pack to

Evan, it'll fall into the hands of someone else just like Curt," Porter said calmly.

"Evan can handle it," Kim snapped.

"No, I can't." Evan stepped into the house behind Porter.

Guess he hadn't left after all.

Panic flooded Kim's face, but she regained composure and made her expression neutral.

"If I take over the pack, people will die. I won't be able to hold on to it. Porter's the best guy for the job," Evan added, his gaze fixed on Kim.

"Hands up," one of the guys growled, and Evan raised his hands to match Porter's. "When he mated with a siren his strength became meaningless."

"That siren saved all of us by offering him her freedom," Evan countered. "You don't need fur to be a part of the pack."

"Just give the pack to Evan so we can get this fucking show on the road," Corbin growled again. "Hand over the pack, or watch your mate lose her head."

"I have no reason to believe that you don't intend to remove her head no matter what I do," Porter said. "I'm not going to be the first one to yield. Let her go, and we can talk about an outcome all of us will agree on."

"If we let her go, you're just going to kill us," the laptop girl argued, finally looking away from the screen.

"If we give in, you could kill her. We can all see the blood on her throat." Evan gestured toward me.

Porter's chest rumbled in anger, the first visible sign of the fury I knew was bubbling beneath his skin.

Silently, I turned up the flow of my magic a little more.

It would make everyone feel warm and a little turned on—but with the intensity of the moment, they would chalk it up to their physical response to what was happening.

I couldn't *really* hit my magic hard until Corbin moved the knife away from my throat.

"Just give Evan the pack," Kim commanded, desperation seeping into her voice. "I'm done watching him spend all of his time with you. He should be with me. We should be in charge. Everything was fine between us before you came back."

The anger—and pain—in her eyes was clear.

She poisoned me and either organized or joined a rebellion because she was *jealous*.

Not jealous that I was mated to Porter.

Jealous that the guy she wanted as her mate had chosen Porter over her since he returned to the pack.

She just wanted time with her fiancé.

It was understandable, until you got to the part where she thought she should betray her alpha rather than working things out with the guy she'd claimed as her mate.

"Kim," Evan said, and he had her complete attention. "If Porter gives me the pack, someone else will challenge me, and I'll lose. Becoming the alpha would kill me. I'm sorry if I've been spending too much time working for the pack, but getting me killed isn't the answer. We can talk. Work things through."

I didn't know if he was serious or not, and I didn't know if Porter would let her leave alive, but he really sold the words.

Tears welled up in Kim's eyes.

"Put the knife down, Corbin," she ordered.

He laughed darkly and pressed it harder to my throat.

"Hit him hard with your magic," Porter commanded, with panic in his voice that didn't show on his face. *"He won't be able to hurt you when it floods him."*

"Are you sure?"

"Positive. Hold the magic until we've dealt with the threat entirely."

I hesitated a moment.

I couldn't feel the effects of my own magic, or my sisters'. I didn't know Corbin, either. I couldn't say for sure how he would respond to the feel of my power.

But Porter knew it intimately, in a way no one else ever had or would.

And I trusted him.

So I tapped into the magic within me, and shoved it into the room. There was no ceremony or flourish—just a thick wave of siren magic.

Corbin groaned, and immediately lowered the knife.

Everyone else made similar noises.

The gun guys dropped their weapons. One started toward me.

The laptop chick leaned against the table she was set up on, arching her back and closing her eyes.

Corbin's knife finally hit the floor.

The moment it did, Porter moved.

The sound of Corbin's spine snapping behind me a moment later made me shudder, violently.

I was basically holding everyone down so he could kill them.

But considering the alternative was to let them kill me, participating was the best choice. I could deal with the mental fuckery of it after I was safe.

While Porter took down Corbin, Evan shifted his nails to claws and tore through the laptop chick's throat, which made me think she was a bigger threat than I'd realized. The other guys had guns, even if their weapons were all on the floor.

Porter and Evan killed them just as fast, negating my theories about them being less of a threat.

Evan's hands were covered in blood when he finally turned to Kim, who was leaning against the wall as she tried to fight my magic. Porter was still physically clean.

For a moment, I saw the uncertainty in Evan's eyes.

He couldn't kill his fiancée.

I knew Porter well enough to be sure he wouldn't let his friend do that.

As expected, my mate set a hand on Evan's shoulder. "I need to question her, to figure out if anyone else is involved. Can you free Izzy?"

Evan jerked his head in a nod.

"Release the magic, baby," he murmured into my mind, meeting my gaze for a moment. The look in his eyes was intense, and full of emotions I couldn't read with the space between us. *"I'm sorry I'm not getting you out of that chair myself, but asking Evan to deal with her is a bad idea."*

"I get it. Thanks for coming after me."

"Always."

Porter made quick work of using Kim's zip ties on her wrists and ankles, positioning her hands in a way that she couldn't use her claws to get herself out.

She tried calling out to Evan for help a few times, but he ignored her.

His hands shook a little as he used his claws to carefully cut through the zip ties holding me to the chair. He pulled a little bit on one around my bicep, and I winced.

"Sorry," he apologized quickly. "I—"

"Don't worry about it. This situation is really screwed up. I don't expect you to have your shit together."

He let out a choked laugh. It was almost a cry.

My heart ached for the guy.

"That's an understatement," he finally said, working through the last two ties. "I didn't know. I would've told Porter. I would've made sure they couldn't hurt you. We've had problems in our relationship since the beginning, but I would've told you if I'd known. I would never let this happen if I could stop it. I—"

"I know." I stood up and set a hand on Porter's arm. Sirens were big on touch, but wolves even more. He would need support. I didn't know him well enough to be that for him, but in the moment, I'd help the only way I could.

He closed his eyes, letting out a shaky breath. "I should've realized."

"No one expects the person they love to do what she did. It's not your fault," I said firmly, stepping toward him and wrapping my arms around him. Porter would probably be a little annoyed, but I knew he would understand in this situation.

Sure enough, before Evan had time to hug me back, Porter

was in the room and squashing me between him and Evan with a hug of his own.

"Your mate's going to smell like me," Evan choked out.

"She already reeks of wolfsbane, vomit, blood, and Corbin. Your scent's basically perfume at this point," Porter grumbled back.

I couldn't suppress a teary laugh.

After a few minutes, Evan finally pulled away. "You should get going. The guys are ready to search this place for evidence of other plans and anyone else who might be involved. I'd like to stay and help."

Porter wrapped an arm around my waist, his grip tight in a way that told me he definitely wasn't feeling as calm as he seemed. "That's fine. We'll take Kim back. I'm assuming you don't want to be involved."

Evan shook his head. "She poisoned your mate and threatened to have her killed out of jealousy. No one should forgive that."

We were in agreement there, even if the warring emotions on his face were much less certain than the ones I felt.

"Let me know when you want an update," Porter said, and Evan nodded. "I won't end her until you decide whether you want a final conversation."

"Thank you."

"Of course."

Porter gave Evan another quick hug, his arm remaining around my waist as he pulled my back to his chest and led me out of the building. It was pitch-black outside, clearly the middle of the night, but there were lights around the house. Porter's truck was waiting in front of us, and the familiarity of it made my chest ache.

There were a half dozen other vehicles there already, with wolves Porter trusted swarming around them. There were so many that even if one or two had been working with Kim, they wouldn't be able to do anything to hurt us.

He ignored the passenger side altogether, carrying me to the driver's and lifting me into the truck. I was in good enough shape that I could've climbed in myself, but I knew he needed to be in control.

As soon as the door shut behind him, he'd set me on his lap, my chest against his. His arms went around my back, his hands slipping beneath my shirt so his palms were on my bare skin. Pressing his nose to my hair, he inhaled deeply, and his chest rumbled angrily.

"Are we driving her back?" I asked him quietly, after a few minutes had gone by. He didn't seem to be calming down, not that I blamed him.

"No. If we were alone with her, I would rip her spine out and feed it down her fucking throat."

His viciousness didn't surprise me. His calmness back in the building had, however.

"They're probably working with more people," I said softly.

"I know. We'll get their names out of her. Everyone will be on their best behavior until then, and I have enough people with her that no one will be able to help her."

I nodded against him.

He let out a slow breath. "I was so fucking terrified."

"I know. Me too. But I'm okay."

"I can smell your blood on your skin, baby."

"If you were a vampire, you'd find it appealing."

He barked out a laugh, shaking his head as his entire body started to tremble "I can't live without you. I survived without my family, just barely—but I can't lose you. I fucking can't."

"You're not going to."

"There's no guarantee."

"We'll just stick together all the time. It's not a big deal."

"You like space, Izzy," he grumbled.

"I like living a lot more. When I need space, I'll make you take me on a hike or a run."

"I can manage that." His arms tightened around me. "I think you're going to have to feed on me, if you want me to turn the truck on. And don't offer to drive—I'm not letting you take the wheel with wolfsbane in your system."

"That's fair." I tipped my head back, and pressed my lips to his. He opened for me after a moment, and I tapped into his emotions.

Fear.

Pain.

Betrayal.

Relief.

As I drank, his emotions deepened.

Desperation.

Possession.

Devotion.

Terror.

Determination.

He was still my buffet. Something told me that would always be the case. The man just felt things more deeply than most people.

We kissed slowly, and I remembered Blair asking me and Avery about Damian's devotion.

About whether or not it could be love.

I'd told her, *"He wants you to be his mate. His real mate. Anyone with eyes can see that."*

She hadn't been sure, because of the way they started out. Damian hadn't given her a choice.

Unlike her, I had chosen to mate with Porter. But that choice didn't come with emotions. It didn't mean he cared about me, or that I cared about him. We had developed those feelings ourselves, over time.

And while our bond had been an emotionless arranged marriage at the beginning, it had become so much more.

I drank until he had become slightly less panicked, and finally pulled away. Wrapping my arms around him, I buried one of my hands in his hair and whispered, "Porter?"

"Yeah?" His hug was fierce.

Warm.

Engulfing, in the very best way.

"You love me," I said.

His chest rumbled. "More than I can fucking take, baby."

"I think I love you too."

"Of course you do. You trust me with your life—and you don't trust anyone like that. Not completely."

My eyes stung.

He was right; I didn't trust anyone with all of my thoughts or feelings. Definitely not all of my emotions. I'd always felt like I had to take care of myself, like no one else would ever be there for me. My parents had ensured that.

But that had changed, if just a little.

Because I trusted Porter.

I trusted him completely.

"You shouldn't have figured that out," I finally said, leaning against him a little bit more.

He dragged his palm lightly over my back. "I can read your emotions through the bond. It makes it pretty easy."

"Cheater."

He chuckled. "I'm mated to a brilliant, gorgeous siren. I need some kind of advantage." He kissed the top of my head. "Ready to go?"

"Yeah. How far are we?"

"A few hours out of Mistwood. This is my cabin. My family's. I lived here, after I abandoned the pack."

I looked at the building with new eyes. Eventually, I wanted to come back and see the place where he'd hidden away for so long, but today obviously wasn't the day. "You didn't abandon them. You left, because they didn't fight for your family."

"I should've stayed," he said, lifting me off his lap and setting me down next to him. "I should've worked through my shit, and stayed."

"Leave the past in the past. You did the best you could with what you knew and understood at the time. And hey, if you stayed, you wouldn't have me."

He started the truck and pulled away from the cabin, onto a well-worn dirt road. "I would've met you at Hale's place and figured out a way to woo you."

I rolled my eyes. "I wouldn't have been wooed, and he wouldn't have let you meet me. Bane is his friend, and he hasn't met any of our sisters."

"Bane doesn't interact with unmated females, and has enough women to protect. He's not interested. I would've been curious, and Hale would've eventually given in."

"The less dark version of you would've liked Clementine more," I countered. "Everyone likes Clem more. She's cute and sweet and happy."

Porter snorted. "As soon as I saw you with your sisters, I knew I wasn't going to mate with anyone but you. If one of them had introduced themselves as my mate, I would've refused, and done whatever it took to convince you to take me. I've never been attracted to anyone the way I am to you."

"Liar."

"Check my emotions. I have no need to lie."

Though I wanted to be confident enough not to do exactly that, I couldn't help but tap in again.

Sure enough, there wasn't a shred of dishonesty.

He'd been attracted to me, and only me, from the beginning.

That was a bit of a turn on.

It would've been a huge one, if not for the events of the day. Err, night? Time felt screwed up.

He pulled one of my legs over his knee, so it was draped over him as he dodged potholes and maneuvered dips in the road like a professional. One of his hands rested on it casually, his massive palm spread over my thigh.

He must've driven the same road a hundred times in the years he'd been gone. Maybe more.

"Do you miss living out here?" I asked him, watching the gorgeous scenery as we drove through.

"No. You know how dark my mind was—this place felt more like a prison than a sanctuary. It reminded me of what I'd lost, every time I opened my eyes."

"And the Manor doesn't?"

"In some ways, it does. But your mind is right up against mine in the pack's link. Thanks to the bond, I'm mentally closer to you than I've ever been to anyone else. Having you close gives me a place to turn when I feel myself falling into the past again."

The words made me warm.

I put my hand on his and squeezed lightly.

He lifted it to his lips and kissed my fingertips. "If I'd lost you, I would've razed the pack to the ground. They would've had to kill me to stop me."

"The only person that wanted me dead was Corbin, and he seemed a little psychotic."

Porter's expression darkened. "He is. I should've hunted him for the way he abandoned my sister. I should've—"

I squeezed his hand again. "It's done. He's gone, and he can't hurt me or anyone else anymore."

He gave a jerky nod. "I just wish it hadn't come to this."

"You're not all-knowing, Porter. You can't see the future or stop all of the bad things and people in the world."

He grimaced, still holding my hand close to his lips. "I didn't protect you any more than I protected them, Izzy."

"Pull over."

He didn't listen.

"Pull over," I repeated.

He reluctantly pulled off the road.

I climbed back onto his lap and put my hands on his face. He grabbed my waist lightly, his expression still dark.

"Look at me, Porter. I'm here. I'm healthy. I still feel like shit —but I'm going to be fine. You found me, and you got me out of there without letting anyone hurt me. And before you bring it up, the cut on my neck is *barely* a scratch."

He scowled, but before he could argue, I continued.

"I never met your family, but I've seen the million pictures of them in our room. I can tell they loved you. I know you love them fiercely. And because of the stories you've shared, I feel like I know who they are. What I know of them makes me absolutely positive that if you could talk to them, they would tell you to stop blaming yourself. You didn't abandon them—you were out of the city because you were helping another pack. Your dad was the one who sent you there. No one could've predicted what happened. It was *not* your fault."

His eyes shone with unshed tears. "It's so fucking unfair, Izzy."

"I know." I caught his single escaped tear with my thumb, wiping it away. "And I'm sorry. But you have to stop blaming yourself. They would want you to be happy, Porter."

He closed his eyes and nodded, his body trembling slightly. "I know."

I released his face and hugged him tightly as he shook against me. The emotions that crashed down on him were so intensely strong that I could feel them with my magic, even though I didn't reach out.

"Tell me we're going to be okay," he said, his voice low and full of emotion.

"We're going to be more than okay. We're going to be powerfully, ridiculously happy. And when the moments of grief hit, we're going to survive it until we feel okay again."

He nodded against me. "I love you."

"I know."

An emotional laugh escaped him, and he hugged me tighter. "Fuck, I'm glad I forced you to marry me."

I laughed. "You couldn't have forced me if I tried. *I* picked *you.*"

"I don't care. I'm just glad you're mine."

We stayed where we were until I finally convinced him to let me take the driver's seat—and he held my thigh like it was his anchor all the way back to the pack's land.

twenty-two

IZZY

THE SUN WAS RISING when we got back. Porter wanted to get me back to our room and take care of me before he dealt with the pack, but I refused. I would survive a few more hours, and the way we dealt with the situation would send a very loud message.

The moment we emerged from the truck, he transformed into the strong, powerful alpha male he always portrayed. Everyone was already gathered together, and he announced without flinching that we'd found the group who wanted me dead.

He warned anyone who might be working with them that we'd captured their leader, and would have the names of anyone else involved before the night was through.

I spent a few hours in a connected room while Porter interrogated Kim. He used his fists to get information out of people sometimes, but he didn't need that with her. There was too much misery in her eyes and there were too many tears streaming down her cheeks.

He told her straight-up that Evan would know whether she gave us answers or not, and she spilled everything without hesitation. He used the pack's link to make sure she was telling the truth, and had someone else taking note of everything she said.

Though I knew he wanted to kill her, Porter walked out when he was sure he had all of the information.

I stuck with him through the rest of the day as he tracked down a handful of traitors who'd tried to run, and killed them. It was gruesome, but necessary. Shifters weren't like humans. They knew the consequences of working against their alpha. He was the leader of their pack family, but he was also their king. They didn't have to like him, and they could leave at any point if they chose to. But helping with a plan to kill his mate was an automatic death sentence.

The sun was setting again when we finally returned to Wolf Manor, stopping in the cafeteria to grab full plates of food on our way.

I expected the pack to be afraid of us, or at least show us the cold shoulder after Porter had ended the lives of some of their packmates, but neither thing was true.

Somehow, everyone was even friendlier.

They thanked us for staying.

Apologized for the traitorous assholes.

Hell, they even gave us more gifts. None of which were edible, they assured us.

They were probably all sex toys, but I had my fingers crossed for more bath bombs. I'd been saving the few I had for a rainy day, and the next few days already felt like they'd be rainy ones.

There were tears in Nora's eyes as she apologized about a hundred times, but it wasn't her fault they'd used the chocolate to poison me. I still wouldn't stop eating chocolate. And Kim had told us who was behind that, so we weren't wondering if Nora was involved.

After I hugged her fiercely and assured her repeatedly that I knew she had nothing to do with it, we finally got our food and made our way out.

"When do you think they'll stop giving me things?" I asked Porter mentally, as we made our way to our room. He was carrying four loaded plates, while my arms were full of gift bags and boxes.

"I don't know. Hopefully never, if it'll make you stay."

I rolled my eyes at him, and he gave me a tired grin.

We were both exhausted.

Back in our room, we sat on the floor together and ate quickly. After we were done, he towed my tired ass to the bathroom, and started filling the tub.

When he dropped the peppermint bath bomb I'd been given

during that first bonfire into the tub, I knew I'd found the perfect man.

He pulled me into the hot water with him, and we both relaxed. With his bare, strong body cradling mine, I didn't think it was possible to get any more comfortable.

We soaked for a while before finally washing up and getting out. Neither of us bothered to grab clothes on our way to the mattress, and we fell asleep curled up in bed together.

It was intimate—but not in a sexual way.

It just made me feel really loved.

I WOKE up with Porter's hand between my legs. It wasn't moving, but his erection throbbed against my thigh in a way that told me he *wanted* to be touching me.

When I lifted my head to look at him with bleary eyes, I realized he was still sleeping.

Honestly, it didn't surprise me in the least that his hand had migrated the way it had.

The man loved my body, whether asleep or awake. There was no way to deny that.

I knew I should let him rest... but a glance at the clock told me we'd already slept to the middle of the afternoon.

So, it would be fine to wake him up.

And he sure as hell wouldn't complain. He loved it when I

woke up horny. Or when I let him have his way with me in the morning.

I pressed his fingers against my clit a little harder, and moved them the way I wanted them. His breathing changed slightly.

I rocked my hips a little, moving against his cock enough to make him groan.

He pulled his hand free of my grasp and dragged me onto his face, making me suck in a breath.

He licked me slowly, and growled. "Fuck, you taste good. Hands on the bed frame, baby."

I set my palms on the wood. My head had collided with the fabric of the canopy over us, but I didn't care.

He licked me from my slit to my ass, and I nearly arched off his face as he brought his fingers to the party, working my clit roughly.

I came hard and fast, rocking against him and crying out loudly. He held me where I was as he gave me one last lick before sliding out from beneath me and rising up at my back. Tilting my hips, he pulled me down hard over his cock until he filled me, making me swear and move against him.

He pinned my hands to the wall as he fucked me from behind, driving into me again and again until I climaxed on his cock, then neared the edge once more. When I unraveled for the third time, his knot finally swelled inside me, making me scream my pleasure as we came together.

Releasing my hands, he pulled my hair to the side of my throat and licked the bite mark he'd left there.

"I need you," he said, one of his hands teasing my breast.

"I'm all yours," I panted.

His chest rumbled, and he bit down on my shoulder slowly.

Carefully.

Gently, even.

It hurt for a moment—and then I was screaming again as another climax hit me, harder than the last.

Porter was mine, and I was his.

And maybe I liked the biting thing more than I realized.

EVENTUALLY, Porter's knot softened and our pleasure faded. He lowered us both to the bed, holding me in his arms as his cock remained inside me, blissfully thick and hard.

We caught our breath together, both of us sweating.

"I'm glad you're a wolf," I mumbled. "Can't beat the knotting thing."

He chuckled against my back. "Good, because I'm all you're going to get, for the rest of your life."

"Sounds fair to me."

"Glad you're so enthusiastic about it."

I laughed.

He chuckled again, kissing my cheek. "You haven't been holding your magic back from me as much as you used to. I love feeling it."

My chest warmed. "Guess I realized I don't need to."

"What made you think you did?"

He wanted to know about my parents, but he wanted to give me an out. We both knew I could just say that sirens were always in danger, and it wouldn't have been a lie.

But I let out a long breath, instead. "My parents were cruel. They weren't abusive, necessarily. They just... didn't like me. Or each other. Or themselves. It wasn't a healthy situation. Maybe they were a little abusive—I don't really know. I've never been able to look at the situation neutrally."

Porter stroked my breasts slowly, the touch more comforting than arousing at the moment.

I went on. "Basically, they just scared and threatened me into keeping my magic under wraps. My dad was a vampire, so they told everyone I was one too. If I ever let my magic free, I was going to be in danger, so they terrified me until I learned to control it. It never felt good, but I was good at it, and they left me alone for the most part when I did. I was grateful for it."

"You shouldn't have had to deal with that," Porter said in a low voice.

"Maybe not, but it could've been worse. Zora... well, she had it worse. My parents were mean, but they didn't hurt me. Not physically, at least."

"No one's going to hurt you now, in any way." Porter kissed my cheek again.

"Except your giant cock."

He snorted. "Except that."

My lips curved upward, and I turned to meet his lips before he could kiss my cheek again. Porter slipped his tongue into my mouth, and I pulled my lower half away from his long enough to roll to my back beneath him.

He slid back inside me, and made slow, sweet love to me once again.

Having a mate was so fucking good.

TWO DAYS LATER, the full moon was set to arrive again.

We were getting ready to spend it together—screwing—when we both got texts calling an emergency meeting for all of the kings.

Ahem, *leaders.*

Some of them still pretended they weren't really royalty.

But apparently Kai had finally emerged from the fae realm, which made it the first time since Porter took over that a full meeting could happen.

We still had a few hours until the moon would officially rise, so we made our way to the neutral territory.

"Have you ever been to one of these meetings before?" I murmured, as we made it through our pack's security doors.

"Nope. It's a first for both of us." He squeezed my hand lightly.

"You know all of the guys pretty well though, right?"

"Hale and Bane, yes. I've met Kai a few times, and we get along fine. Talon, I don't know well."

"He's the one who keeps saying he needs a siren. Apparently, Clementine is thinking about mating with him," I murmured.

Porter's eyebrows lifted. "That would be a terrible idea. The bastard would break her."

"I know. It seems like something must be going on with his dragons that he doesn't want to admit. I think my other sisters talked her out of mating with him, but she's looking for something sexy and exciting."

"If she wants sexy and exciting, she should join the pack for the full moon. She'd have as many partners as she wanted, and none of them would be in their right mind enough to try to claim her because of her magic."

"I'll offer, but I don't think she'll take me up on it. I told them how rough full moon sex is supposed to be."

I sent her a quick text, but she didn't answer before I had to put my phone away as we reached the room the meeting would take place in.

Porter nodded at the vampire and dragon guards at the doors, and we stepped through.

My gaze moved quickly over the room. It was big and open, with five couches spread apart but forming a wide circle. There were bookshelves and armchairs on the outsides of the room, so it wasn't bare, but the couches were obviously the most important part.

One of them held a gorgeous man with light skin and blond hair that looked wildly overgrown. He was draped out across the length of it, his chest rising and falling slowly.

Apparently, he was sleeping.

The vines growing around his arms and the couch while he was unconscious told me that he was Kai, the fae king.

Another chair held a big, angry-looking bastard with light brown skin and black hair that fell to his cheekbones. He was sitting up, his arms folded and his position tense.

Definitely Talon.

His eyes tracked me closely, but the mark on my throat ensured my safety.

Porter wouldn't have let him take me even without the mate mark, so I was safe either way.

Another set of doors opened across from us, and Porter

relaxed slightly as the biggest man I'd ever seen came striding into the room.

His lips curved upward when he saw my mate, and Porter led me into the middle of the space so he could give the other guy a bro hug.

Obviously, this was Bane.

He had tan skin and shaggy, wavy hair that looked like it had a hand run through it far too many times.

"Good to have you back," Bane said, as he released Porter.

"It's good to be back," Porter admitted. "This is my mate, Izzy. Izzy, this is Bane."

I gave him a quick smile, but the doors behind us opened again before I had to come up with a conversation.

"I told you we were late," Blair murmured, barely loud enough for me to hear. Her cheeks were red and her lips were swollen, but she looked ridiculously happy.

"He's always late," Talon said flatly.

"It's a tradition," Hale drawled, leading his mate to one of the couches. They both sat down, and we walked with Bane to the others. When he moved toward one of the last two, it was clear which one belonged to us, so we went that way.

Blair mouthed, *"Damn, you look happy,"* to me, and I rolled my eyes at her even though I couldn't suppress a smile.

Her smile widened too.

"We don't have much time before the full moon," Porter said, setting his hand on my thigh.

"I think we have plenty of time to talk about how Hale gave you one of his sirens but won't give me one," Talon said, setting his glare on Porter.

"I don't know what you're talking about," I said. "I heard that the vampire king had a siren mate and assumed he would keep me safe while I was unmated. When they told me I could mate with the next wolf king to guarantee my safety, I agreed readily. You know sirens believe in arranged marriage."

Talon scoffed and opened his mouth.

"We're not here to talk about sirens," Bane said, cutting Talon off. "If you're ready to ask for help, we'll help you. Until then, we need to focus on the fae. Kai?" He looked at the sleeping king.

The rest of us did too.

Bane repeated his name, louder, and the man finally jerked into a sitting position, his eyes bleary.

Fuck, he was pretty.

I wasn't interested in pretty—but there could be no denying the appeal he would have for some women.

He snapped a vine as he tugged his arm free and ran a hand over his face. "Sorry. Haven't slept in a while. We're going through our worst eclipse yet, and there's no end in sight. I think I can push it to wrap up, but I'd need to tap into the rest of my fae's magic to push the eclipse toward its end."

I had no idea what to say to that.

The silence throughout the room told me no one else did, either.

"I need them sane for that," he explained. "And the eclipse keeps them from sanity."

"So you need them sane to stop the eclipse, but because of it, you can't get them sane?" Hale summarized.

"Yes." He looked at me and Porter.

Something told me we weren't going to like what was coming next.

"I need your lake."

"No," Porter said, without consideration.

Kai's eyes narrowed.

"Permanently?" Blair checked. "You can't take a siren's water source permanently. That's never going to fly with one of us, or our mate."

"And the pack isn't going to give up any part of our territory for good," Porter said.

Kai shook his head. "Just for tonight. Your water eases the effects almost completely for the fae who swim there. If I can get enough of them into your lake, I think I can end the eclipse for now."

I relaxed a little.

"Are you good with that?" Porter asked me.

"Yeah, we should help them if we can. As long as they're not going to hurt the pack."

"If anything, the pack will have more fun with fae running around while the moon's up. But it's your lake, so you set the rules."

"It's the full moon tonight," I said, looking back at Kai. "You're welcome to use it, as long as you're not going to hurt any of our wolves or have a problem with them running wild."

"That's not a problem. We're basically dealing with the same situation, so the fae will be more interested in gathering during your full moon anyway. I'll make the call."

"Izzy and I won't be out in the forest, so if anything goes wrong, it's on you," Porter added. "And don't kill the fish."

"I'll take the blame, and the fish will be fine," Kai agreed. "Thank you."

There was genuine gratitude in his eyes that made me glad we could help, even if just by loaning out my lake. We'd be locked in our bedroom, so it wasn't like we would be using it anyway.

"Any other problems?" Bane asked, looking around the group.

"I still need a siren," Talon grumbled.

"And it's still not happening unless you actually tell us what's going on," Bane said firmly.

Talon clenched his fists, standing and striding out of the room.

"He didn't used to be that much of an asshole," Hale remarked, after the door was shut behind him.

"Something is obviously happening, but he's going to have to swallow his pride and talk to us if he wants help," Bane said, standing too. "Good luck with the eclipses, and the full moon."

He strode out of the door he'd come through.

Porter shuddered, and I looked over as he let out a slow breath.

Full moon incoming.

"We have to go," I said, looking back at Kai. "There are no guards on duty when the moon is up, just keep your distance from any mean-looking wolves. No killing."

"Got it." He rose to his feet. "I'll be in and out before the moon's effects wane."

"Perfect." I flashed him a smile, mouthed, "Talk soon," to Blair, and towed my mate out of the room before he lost control of his instincts and started screwing me against the nearest wall or something.

We wove through the hallways quickly, but Porter shuddered again, harder, before we reached the room.

He halted abruptly, a few halls away from our space.

Shit.

I watched his eyes change as the moon's effects settled on him, and an idea struck me.

Wolves had major chase instincts. Even with the moon weighing him down, I could use that.

"Porter," I said, taking a few steps backward.

He stepped with me immediately.

I flashed him a grin. "I'll meet you in our room."

I turned, and *ran*.

With my vampire speed, he didn't stand a chance at keeping pace with me, but he reached our bedroom less than twenty seconds after I did. I made a show of trying to close the door to our room, as if I was going to lock him out, but he muscled it open and smashed his way in.

Heady male pride shone through his wolfy eyes as he locked the door behind us.

I couldn't stop my lips from curving upward as his gaze moved down my body predatorily.

He stalked me through the room, and I stepped backward until my ass met the wall.

There would be no real running from him.

Not while the moon was up.

"You're mine," Porter said, his voice all wolf.

"Am I?"

His eyes flashed with warning as he reached me. "Don't push me, mate."

"Or what?"

His gaze darkened, and he pressed me into the wall. His nails were sharpened to claws, but I didn't think he'd noticed. "Or you'll wear my release on those pretty little lips."

"Doesn't sound like much of a threat, Porter."

He lifted a hand to my shirt and slowly tore through the fabric, cutting both it and my bra down the middle. He pushed the fabric open, and dragged a claw lightly over one of my nipples, making me shiver.

"I'm in charge tonight. Understand?"

"What if I don't?"

His eyes flashed.

In a heartbeat, he had my pants and thong down my thighs and was thrusting inside me, hard.

My lips parted with a gasp, my hands landing on his shoulders as he fucked me roughly, dragging me to the edge fast. Before I could come, he pulled out.

And pushed me slowly to my knees.

I was panting when he pressed his cock to my lips, the length of it wet with my own slickness.

"Open," Porter said.

I did.

He thrust into my mouth slowly, stopping before it grew uncomfortable for me. He worked himself in and out, letting me suck him and touch him until his cock was throbbing as he fought back his release.

"Tell me what I want to hear, mate," he commanded, still fully possessed by his beastly instincts as he pulled out of my mouth enough to let me speak.

"I'm yours," I said, desire making me drenched.

The game was over.

I just wanted him to screw me.

"And."

"And you're in charge tonight."

Victory glittered in his eyes.

"You knew that even without me saying it, tho—oh!" I shrieked as he yanked me off the floor. I was pinned to the wall again a moment later as he fucked me harder than before.

All thoughts died as he pushed me into the first of many climaxes.

Maybe I loved the full moon.

twenty-three

IZZY

WHEN I EVENTUALLY WOKE UP AND tried to climb out of bed the next morning, Porter dragged me back in and kissed me.

Hard.

His mouth still tasted like my pleasure, which turned me on all over again.

I'd gone to sleep thinking I'd never be horny again, but that had clearly been wrong.

An hour later, we finally made it out of bed and to the shower. I thought about fishing my phone out of my pants —I was pretty sure it was still in the pocket—but Porter scooped me up off my feet before I could.

I laughed, meeting his heart-stopping grin with my own smile as he carried me back to the tub.

Maybe I'd started a new obsession for him.

"I ordered you more bath bombs yesterday," he said, kissing the claim mark on my shoulder as he started the water.

"You ordered *you* more bath bombs?" I teased.

"I ordered *us* more bath bombs."

I snorted, and he chuckled, kissing my shoulder again. "What do you want to do today? The pack will be lazing around, so we're free. We have the pack's Thanksgiving celebration tomorrow, because we always do it a day early. The day after that, we celebrate with your sisters and Hale in Vamp Manor."

"So we need to have our fun today, because we'll be busy the rest of the week?" I asked.

"Right." He kissed me on the lips, distracting me for a long moment.

"Maybe we should—"

Someone knocked loudly on our door.

I frowned at Porter.

His forehead creased.

I knew he'd be quickly checking the pack, to see if something had gone wrong.

"Everything's fine with the wolves," he said, reaching for a towel.

"You are *not* answering our door in a towel." I strode toward the door with him hot on my heels, grabbing his shirt off the floor.

"If I'm not answering in a towel, you're not answering in my shirt." He reached for my waist to stop me, but the person at the door knocked louder.

"Izzy!" A feminine voice yelled from the other side of the door.

It was so muffled, I couldn't tell which one of my sisters it was, but I knew in my gut that it was one of them.

Porter didn't try to stop me as I rushed to the door, yanking it open. Zora was on the doorstep, her expression panicked.

"What happened?" I demanded.

She surged into the room, shoving a hand through her wild curls. "Clem snuck out of Vamp Manor last night. She left a note in her room. I tried to call you when I found it a few hours ago, but you didn't answer. She said she was coming here, to hang out with the pack during the full moon. Did you see her? I know she wanted to hook up with a werewolf, but—"

"Fuck. I invited her. I forgot I invited her." I lifted a hand to my forehead. "She could be in bed with a wolf right now.

"Maybe, but she's not answering her phone."

"I wasn't answering my phone."

"You're mated," she pointed out. "And you knew no one would be looking for you."

"The fae were here," Porter said in a low voice. "We didn't tell her."

"We didn't know when we invited her."

"What do you mean, the fae were here?" Zora demanded. "She said it was safe, because the wolves would be controlled by the moon."

"It would've been. If she didn't find the fae. Fuck," I shoved a hand over my hair. "This is my fault."

Porter found his jeans on the floor, and pulled his phone out.

"She should've told someone she was leaving," Zora said, her panic rising. "What if one of the fae took her to their realm to force her to mate with them?"

"Hey, Kai," Porter growled into the phone, then paused. "Where is he?"

Zora and I both hurried toward him.

He pulled the phone away from his ear and put it on speaker. "Say that again."

"While Kai was trying to end the eclipse last night, a group of fae found an unmated siren swimming with them. Kai recognized her as one of the vampire queen's sisters just as one of the fae took her into our realm. He disappeared after her."

"Can he bring her back?" Zora demanded.

The guy paused, probably surprised to realize someone else was listening to his call.

"Not until she's mated," the man admitted. "But he's trying to find her a mate so he can bring her back. He doesn't want war."

Panic flooded Zora's face as she gripped her hair again, not caring even a little about the tangled wreck that her curls had become.

"Shit," Porter said, closing his eyes.

"Yeah, we're pretty fucked on this side of things too. The eclipse still hasn't ended." Someone yelled something on his side of the call, and the guy groaned. "I've got to go. I'll call you back when I hear from Kai. It shouldn't take long for him to find your mate's sister someone to bond with. Hopefully, they'll be back today."

With that, he hung up the phone.

"Holy hell," I murmured, my hand still on my forehead.

"What the fuck was she thinking?" Zora demanded, then pinned her glare on me. "What the fuck were *you* thinking?"

"I never heard back from her, okay? I would've felt my phone vibrate if she texted me before we got back for the full moon. Obviously, I was a little preoccupied with my mate and the magic of everything." I grabbed my pants off the floor and pulled out my phone, turning the screen on.

I'd missed a dozen calls from Zora, a few from Avery, and one from Blair, but there was just a single text from Clementine. She hadn't messaged me back until nearly 1 AM, hours after the full moon's effects had kicked in.

I handed it to Zora, and she read the messages.

ME

Hey! It should be safe for you to join the pack during one of our full moons if you ever want to get out of Vamp Manor and have some fun with a wolf. Just let me know if you're ever interested, and I'll do what I can to make it happen

Love you!

CLEM

I'm lonely, think I'm going to head over there tonight! Don't worry about making it happen, I'll figure it out ;) Love you too!

Zora groaned. "What is wrong with her?"

"She wants a mate."

"Well, now she's getting one. I sincerely hope Kai can find her someone who will treat her right, or we're going to have to kill her *actual mate* this time."

"Kai's a decent guy, and he knows his people can't afford a war right now. He'll make sure she's with someone who can protect her," Porter said.

"Let's cross our fingers," Zora said, hitting the button on her phone to call Avery.

She updated her—and all three of us ended up heading over to Vamp Manor, to figure out if there was anything else we could do for her.

. . .

AFTER SPENDING the better part of the day pacing and arguing, we all finally admitted to ourselves that there was nothing we could do for Clementine except wait.

Zora was sincerely thinking about mating with a fae herself just so she could find and protect Clem, but thankfully, we talked her out of it.

Eventually, Porter and I made it back to our room.

"I'm sorry," he said, frustration in his voice as we got back in bed together. "I should've remembered that we invited her."

"It's not our fault. Clem was lonely. She had been thinking about taking a mate anyway. At least this way, we know Kai will mate her with someone who can keep her safe. He won't want to piss us off," I said, though worry for her had my stomach clenching too.

"And at least she didn't offer herself up to Talon," Porter said.

A sharp laugh escaped me. "No kidding."

He stroked my arm lightly, and I leaned against him, resting my eyes. "I hope she has an adventure. She could have the time of her life over there, with the right person."

"I hope so too," Porter admitted, still tracing lines on my arms.

I tried to doze off, but couldn't get my mind off of Clementine.

"Need a distraction?" he asked me.

"Yes, but I'm not horny."

"Neither am I." He hesitated a moment before asking, "Have you ever thought about kids? Having kids? With me?" The way he tripped over the words made my lips curve upward.

"Maybe. Have you?"

"Yes. I don't think I'm ready yet, but I'd like to have a handful of them. I want to build a family. I don't know if I'd be a good dad, but—"

"You'd be an amazing dad," I said quietly.

"Thank you." He continued tracing on my arm. "All the kids here love you. Watching you play with them always makes me itch to knock you up."

I laughed. "I didn't know that was an itch."

"For a guy? Oh, yeah. I already have big dreams about fucking you while you're pregnant."

A snort escaped me. "That does *not* sound sexy."

"The sexy part is that you'll be round with our daughter, baby."

"Or our son."

"Mmhm." He let out a long breath. "Sounds too good to be true. I haven't let myself think about having kids in a long, long time."

"You wanted them before the attack?"

"Yeah. I was looking for a mate, but it was difficult."

"Because of your dad's rule about business and pleasure?"

He chuckled. "Partially. And I just didn't find the right woman."

"Well, I hope I'm the right one, because there's no going back now."

"You're perfect, Izzy." He leaned over and kissed my nose. "Isabella."

"Do you want me to punch you?"

He grinned.

"You never told me if we're business or pleasure," I remarked.

"We're both. I always knew I'd screw that rule when I found the right person."

"Literally," I drawled, earning a chuckle.

"Over and over again." He slid his finger between my breasts and toward my core before trailing it back up and to my arm.

"I'd like to have a big family, some day," I admitted quietly. "I love my sisters. If we have kids, I want them to have as many siblings as I do. Or more. Even though that idea is terrifying when it comes to the part where I have to grow the babies."

"I'll feed you chocolate until they pop out. You won't even notice how much it sucks."

I smiled. "Is that a yes to a big family?"

"Of course it is. You know family is everything to me. And now, you're that." He kissed my nose again, and I pulled his lips down to mine, kissing him lightly.

"My sisters have to be your family too."

"Of course. I'm going to give the bastards who mate with them an obligatory punch to the face. Hale will help"

"That sounds like a good way to scare them off."

"It's what brothers are for."

"Knowing Clem, she'll be determined to make it work, even if we can all tell it's a toxic shitshow."

"Have a little faith, baby."

"I do. I just don't want to get my hopes up for her, and feel guilty all over again."

"A mate bond is whatever you make it. We proved that, didn't we?"

"I guess we did." I slipped my fingers into his hair, and he closed his eyes as I played with the strands lightly. "I love you."

"I love you too."

"Let's practice making a baby tomorrow, okay?"

He grinned. "And every day after."

"Deal."

Porter leaned over to kiss me, and I didn't hesitate to kiss him back.

I'd helped him free himself from the darkness—and I would never let him go back.

Hell, I would never let him go at all.

I loved him, and the life we'd started to make together, too fucking much to ever consider that. Life would never be easy... but we didn't need easy.

We had each other.

And that was all that really mattered.

THANKSGIVING with the pack went smoothly.

Evan said his goodbyes to Kim, and I ended her life without ceremony. It may have been cruel to do so, but I couldn't allow someone who would poison and abduct my mate to live.

He buried himself in pack work and paperwork, and I left him be. He was going to need time to heal. A lot of time. But I wouldn't let him sink into the darkness of the place I'd been.

There were no remaining threats to my mate, so I could finally breathe a little easier. I'd never stop watching, after what happened to my family, but I wouldn't let myself obsess over it.

We headed over to Vamp Manor on the actual holiday, and Izzy held my hand tighter than she usually did.

"I used to think I wouldn't like holding someone's hand," she admitted to me, as we made our way through the vampires' security checkpoint.

"Why?"

"I don't know. I guess it seemed silly. Now I hold your hand all the time." She shrugged.

I could tell she was nervous, and trying to distract herself.

"What are you worrying about?" I asked, pulling her a little closer.

She sighed. "Without Clem there, everything will be different. Blair's sort of the leader, and I'm like, the sarcastic, independent one, but Clementine holds us together. We were all quiet and sad when she was stuck in Vamp Manor before the rest of us were allowed in. I'm worried it will be like that again."

"We'll try to make the best of it," I said, squeezing her hand.

"And if it's awkward?"

"Then we feign being tired from the pack's holiday, and call it a night early."

She smiled, though she still looked worried. "I guess that's as good a plan as any."

"It'll be fine, baby." I kissed her as the elevator closed behind us.

We met everyone else in a large meeting room close to Hale's office. Though Zora still looked angry and was keeping to herself, everyone else was chatting. We greeted Hale's sister and her mate, along with a few other vampires I vaguely recognized as people who were close with Hale. One of them was a doctor. Kara, maybe?

Despite Izzy's worries, she settled into a conversation about the pack easily enough.

When the doors flew open a few minutes later, all of us turned our heads.

Izzy sucked in a breath beside me when an irritated-looking Clementine strode into the room with a blond fae man behind her.

"Tell me she didn't mate with the fae king," Avery whispered to Zora, behind us.

"I don't think I can," Zora groaned.

Something told me there was a pretty good story behind that—and I looked forward to hearing it.

Tucking my mate against my side, I flashed Kai a small grin. "Welcome to the family."

PORTER—AT SOME POINT IN THE FUTURE

"STOP STALLING, Iz. Just pee on the stick."

"I told you, I'm not peeing in front of you," she tossed back, waving the stick with her as she gestured toward the door. "Get out."

"I'm a wolf, baby. We pee on things to mark them as our territory. It's a miracle I haven't peed on *you* yet. Let's get this over with." I waved her toward the toilet.

Her face was red. "What if it's negative again? I could just be losing my mind. I've already had a dozen negative tests, and I think I'm going to lose it if this one's negative too. People lose their minds when they try for babies. It's a thing, okay? I don't want to be crazy. I—"

I kissed her hard, then pulled away. "If you're crazy, we'll deal with it. If you're not pregnant, we'll keep screwing until you are, the same way we always do. We can't control what the test says, but it'll happen when the time is right. Either way, it's time to learn the answer."

She sighed dramatically. "If you leave me because I'm crazy, I *will* kill you."

"I like you crazy. Stop stalling."

"Fine. At least look away."

I did as she requested, turning my head as she did the deed.

When the toilet flushed, I grabbed the stick from her hand. She'd already capped the top of it, so the thing was close enough to clean.

"You're supposed to put it on the countertop. Don't tip it down like that. I've read the instructions like a hundred times," she said, swiping it from my hand and setting it down.

"How long do we wait again?" I peered at the little window, where the lines were supposed to appear.

"Three minutes. One line means not pregnant. Two lines means pregnant."

"What if there are three lines?"

"That's not how it works. And it hasn't been long enough. Distract me, please."

I stepped back, pulling her between me and the countertop and opening her thighs with my knee. She leaned her weight against it, then plopped her face against my bicep. "I don't want it to be negative. I hate seeing the negatives."

We'd been trying for a baby for nearly a year, and it had been hard on Izzy.

So fucking hard on her.

I felt like shit every time I saw her try not to cry, but there was nothing I could do except hold her close and tell her I loved her.

And fuck her, again.

"It's normal for a couple to take up to a year to get pregnant, baby. We're normal."

"Normal sucks," she whispered, and I felt her tears leak through my shirt.

I pulled her close, looking back at the window. If it was negative, I'd need to prepare her. Fuck her against the countertop so it wouldn't hurt as bad, or something.

But when I saw it, my heart nearly stopped.

"Izzy," I said.

"Don't look at it. I don't want to know."

"Izzy," I repeated, my voice lower.

"Do *not* get my hopes up. The last thing I want to do is cry again."

"Look at the test, baby."

She spun around, and froze.

Just stood there, and stared.

Her hand was shaking as she picked up the test, staring at the window.

"Two lines," she said, her voice faint. "I've never seen two lines before."

"You're pregnant, Iz."

"I'm pregnant," she breathed.

"You're fucking pregnant!"

"Holy shit. Holy shit. Holy shit!" She flung her arms around me, and I hauled her off the ground as I hugged her tightly. "I love you so much," she said into my shoulder, her eyes watering again. "I can't believe it."

"Believe it, baby. We're going to be parents."

Her gaze met mine, those beautiful eyes bright with deep, fierce emotions. "I love you so much."

"I love you too."

I did.

I loved her so much, it hurt.

She was the perfect mate for me, and she'd be the perfect mom for our kids.

She'd saved my life—and I was going to make her as happy as I fucking could for the rest of ours, together.

afterthoughts

Wow.
So this book was a little more serious than I thought it would be.
I probably should've put it together, with Porter being the grieving alpha and Izzy being the independent sister who dealt with her own crap, but I didn't.
Despite that, it made me feel really hopeful. Because we all struggle, but we all have tools to help us through grief— even if they aren't quite as sexy as sirens in bikinis ;)
And no matter how dark things get, we can all find our way back.
Life sucks sometimes, but we're strong enough to make it through. Stronger than we realize.
There's a quote I love that says, "if it's not okay, it's not the end."
So if things aren't okay for you right now, just keep going.
You can and will make it through.

And if you're just here for the fun, buckle up for the next
book, because Clem's story is going to be a reallll good time
;)
All the love,
Lola Glass <3

stay in touch

If you want to receive Lola's newsletter for new releases (no spam!) use this link:

LINK

Or find her on:
FACEBOOK
TIKTOK
INSTAGRAM
PINTEREST
GOODREADS

Shifter City

Supernatural Underworld

Moon of the Monsters

Rejected Mate Refuge

Lola is a book lover with a *slight* romance obsession and a passion for love. Especially love between sassy women and huge, growly magical men;)
When she's not reading or writing up a storm, she's hanging out with her husband and two little boys, or baking something sugary that she *probably* shouldn't eat (but will).